I0620697

FERNANDO
By Chanel Hardy

Hardy Publications

ISBN-13: 978-1735107301

Printed in the United States of America

"I knew even as a teenager that my femininity was more than just adornments; they were extensions of me, enabling me to express myself and my identity. My body, my clothes and my makeup are on purpose, just as I am on purpose."

-Janet Mock

Fernando

Prologue

Winter, 1997

Knots formed in the center of Amari's abdomen as she sat on the hospital bed. Soon she would be transferred to the operating room. Her mother Elise stood by her side, grasping her daughters' hand. Elise bowed her head, closed her eyes and spoke softly as she prayed over Amari. After nearly three years of puberty blockers and hormone replacement therapy, it was finally Amari's big day. Getting bottom surgery would mark the beginning of her new life as a fully transitioned transgender woman.

"I can't believe this is actually happening." Amari said. She placed her hand over her stomach. "I'm so nervous."

"Don't be," Elise said. "I'm here. Everything will be fine." Elise smiled and rubbed Amari's shoulder.

It had taken a long time for Elise to come to terms with her daughter's transition. At the age of thirteen, Amari came out as trans to her mother. Elise found breast pads and a tote bag full of makeup hidden in Amari's closet, which led to an emotional breakdown that caused a huge rip in their relationship.

With a lack of support, Amari disobeyed her mother and turned to the street life. She committed petty crimes to afford her hormone medication. The first time Amari was caught shoplifting, Elise found hormone pills in her room. At that moment, she realized that what her daughter was going through was no phase. She set her own feelings aside and decided that she would provide the support Amari needed on her journey to transition, even if she didn't understand it.

"Have you heard from dad?" Amari asked.

Amari looked up at her mother with hopeful eyes. Elise didn't respond. She just nodded with pressed lips. Amari let out a faint sigh.

While her father was supportive of her coming out as queer, he wasn't too fond of her coming out as trans. He was even more opposed to her having such a life-changing procedure. Amari felt that he would always subconsciously hold on to the son he always wanted. But despite his opposition, she was having the surgery with or without him.

"He loves you." said Elise as she reassured Amari. "You know that."

"I know." replied Amari. She smiled weakly.

Someone knocked on the door. Elise and Amari looked to see who was there.

"Are we ready to go?" asked a male voice. The doctor peeked his head inside the patient room.

"Yes." Amari answered. Her stomach settled as the excitement for her new life set in.

The doctor walked in and approached them with his clipboard in hand.

"Good." said the doctor. "Let's get you prepped for surgery."

Amari laid back and still held on to her mother's hand as the doctor prepared to take her into surgery. They locked eyes. Elise placed her palm on her daughter's chin. This was it.

"Damarion Davis." a male voice called out. Two men approached the room door. One, being a uniformed police officer. A sharp pain pierced Amari's chest. Her skin prickled.

"Excuse me?" Elise interjected. She inched closer towards Amari. "What do you want with my daughter?" Her brow furrowed as she observed the two men.

"I'm Detective Porter." said the man in regular clothes. As he reached into his blazer to pull out his badge, he stared down Amari. "Damarion, you are under arrest for theft and credit card fraud." The uniformed officer reached for his cuffs and proceeded to Amari.

"What is the meaning of this?" Elisa questioned in a fretful tone. She peered down at her daughter. "Amari, what is happening?"

The look of guilt and regret washed over Amari's face as the officer sat her up and placed the cuffs on her wrists. Her eyes glossed with tears as her whole world imploded. She was so close to starting a new life, and just like that, it was all over before it began.

Chapter 1

One year, six months later…

I sat in front of my vanity mirror and wiped the burgundy lipstick from my lips with a napkin. I picked up a nude brown shade and carefully applied it to my full lips. "That's the Way Love Goes" by Janet played through my radio, blasting at full volume. The music put me in a tranquil mood. I puckered my lips and ran my index finger over my perfectly shaped brows. I didn't have many skills that were worth bragging about, but my true talent shined in hair and makeup. I adjusted my bra straps. Then, I ran my palms over the lace that covered my 32B sized breasts. They had grown naturally after four years of hormone therapy. My breasts were my biggest pride and joy. and they represented the womanhood that I desperately desired. My journey to transition was cut short when a judge sentenced me to a year in Woodson County jail for theft and credit card fraud. I told my mother that I had gotten a part-time job to come up with the money needed to pay for my surgery. But no low-paying entry-level job could pay for a $23,000 procedure. The day I was arrested was the worst day of my life. My crimes had finally caught up to me. What would've been a minimum of five years in federal prison was reduced to only a misdemeanor. Thanks to my father's connections, I was able to get a good lawyer. It also helped that I had a clean record prior to my arrest. Also, I cooperated with detectives to turn on one of the men I was working with.

But a year in a men's jail felt like an eternity for me. The violence and sexual abuse I had to endure was a living hell until I decided to stop being a victim. I used my feminine looks and street smarts to my advantage. It had its benefits, which included getting black market hormone pills smuggled in. Surviving in jail came with a cost, but my rigid character could get me though anything.

There was a knock at my bedroom door.

"May I come in?" asked my mother in a muffled voice.

"Yeah." I answered as I paused my music.

My mother opened the door and peered in before she eased her way inside. She walked over to where I sat and stood next to me. She pushed my hair behind my shoulder and smiled at me though the mirror.

"Is that a new lip color?" she asked.

"Yeah, I got it yesterday." I said flatly. I put all my makeup back in its place before turning off my vanity light. "Don't worry. I paid for it." I rolled my eyes.

My mother scoffed. "I never said you didn't." She tilted her head and placed her hand on my shoulder. "What's with the attitude today?"

I sighed heavily. "This Brazil trip is starting to feel like a bad idea. I don't even speak Spanish. I don't know anyone there except dad."

"They speak Portuguese in Brazil. I'm sure you won't be the only one speaking English there." My mother leaned down and hugged me tightly. "I know you're nervous, but you'll make friends. I know it." She placed a gentle kiss on my temple.

"We'll see." I said unenthusiastically.

"Yes, you will." My mother smiled. "Now hurry and finish getting ready. I want to make it to the airport before rush hour."

She left my room, and I turned my music back on as I got up and stepped away from my vanity. I went over to my bed where a black sundress with red roses sat across the end of it. It was my favorite, and one of the first outfits I bought when my breasts started to develop. The V-neck with wide straps complimented my small frame perfectly. Since it wasn't too tight below the waist, I didn't have to worry about tucking either. I didn't mind it usually. I had been doing it since I started wearing feminine clothing at thirteen-years-old. But summertime in the south wasn't exactly ideal weather for wearing duct tape, and I couldn't wear it for long periods of time, even if I wanted to.

Sundresses gave me the freedom to be comfortable without attracting too much unwanted attention. Most people I encountered didn't know I was trans. My mother pulled me out of public school not too long after I started hormone therapy. Homeschooling helped keep me safe from bullies but living in Montgomery Georgia as a queer person was risky regardless of how much I tried to shelter myself. I felt like the more I could pass as a cisgender woman, the easier my life would be until I could get my surgery.

My narrow nose and small cheekbones did make it easier, but the puberty blockers and hormone therapy gave me the privilege of passing that kept my gender identity from being questioned by strangers. I was so close, and what felt like my only chance at having the life I truly wanted was taken away the day I was arrested.

My eyes became glossy with tears as flashbacks from the day my whole world came crashing down replayed in my mind. I tossed my dress over my head and wiped a tear that emerged from my eyelid. I refused to let my past kill my spirits. There was nowhere to go but forward, and these next few months in Brazil would be the beginning of a fresh start for me.

Chapter 2

Fifteen hours and two flights later, I had finally arrived at Campina Grande Airport. Rubbing my aching backside, I inhaled and exhaled heavily as I made my way to baggage claim to meet my father Marcus. It had been three years since we had last seen each other. He left for the Peace Corps when I was sixteen years old. Although he and my mother had been divorced since I was eight years old, I still maintained a relationship with my father. Despite his issues with my transition, we tried to make it work.

With my carry-on bag draped over my shoulder, I looked at my surroundings as I walked through the airport. I hadn't even been outside yet, and it was already a culture shock. The sounds of a foreign language filled my ears as travelers, walking by, carried on with their conversations. A slight feeling of butterflies arose in my stomach as I headed down the escalator to approach the baggage claim area. As I reached the bottom, my father stood by the luggage carousel. I spotted his tall frame and red baseball hat as he held the handles of my suitcases in each hand. He spotted me almost immediately. My blank expression left as my eyes gleamed at the sight of my father, smiling back at me as I walked to him.

"Hey kiddo!" he called out. He let go of the suitcase handles to embrace me.

"Hey, daddy!" I cheered. I dropped my bag and ran into his arms to give him a hug.

My father broke our embrace. "I'm so glad you agreed to come here." He observed me as he held the sides of my arms. "You look nice." He ran his hand over my long, wavy hair. "I like this hairstyle on you. What kind of hair is it? I don't know what Y'all are wearing these days?"

"Dad." I whined, gently swatting his hand away. "Thanks for the compliments but you don't have to try so hard." I chuckled faintly. His need to overcompensate was annoying.

The corner of his mouth raised slightly, his hand hung from my shoulder. "Alright, let's get you out of here." He took my carry-on, tossing the strap over his shoulder and clutching the handles of my suitcases as we headed for the exit.

***

The hot and humid summer air brushed against my arm as I gazed out of the open passenger side window. Natal was a small costal city on the eastern side of Brazil. The long landscape of big green trees along the small roads reminded me of home. Once we reached the inner city, the scenery felt more familiar as we passed a Toyota dealership.

"It kind of looks like home." I said as I observed the locals riding by on the road next to us. Others walking along on the sidewalks.

"Well yeah." Said my father. "What did you expect? Dirt roads and people carrying buckets of water on their heads?" My father laughed.

I turned to him. "No. I mean… I didn't really know what to expect."

"There are homes, stores, restaurants. Just like back home. The culture is different, but as long as you stay out of trouble, you'll be fine. Natal is great. Don't worry, you'll like it. I've already got a position set up for you to volunteer on the job site."

I scoffed. "I've been here for an hour and you're already talking about work."

"I don't want to hear it. My father gently tapped the steering wheel. You already know the deal." This isn't a vacation for you. It's a break for your mother."

"Right. Mom is the one who needs a break." I leaned back against my seat, slouching with my arms folded.

"Everything's not always about you." He glanced over at me. "This is exactly why I want you working with me. Lucky for you, having a federal job with the corps has its perks. I was able to pull some strings for you. The Peace Corps has really changed my life. I know it'll change yours too."

"Mm hmm. Whatever." I mumbled. I continued to look out the window. Dad wasn't like my mother. Things that she let me get away with wouldn't fly under his roof.

"Since you want to have a smart mouth, you'll start first thing tomorrow morning."

"What? Half the day is already gone! I just got here!"

"Too bad." He turned up the music on the radio, bringing the conversation to an abrupt end. I clenched my jaw, glaring at my father. My nostrils flared. I slouched down in my seat, wondering why I ever agreed to this. The last thing either of us wanted was to spend the next three months being at each other's throats. But I could already feel the discontentment he had towards me emanating from him. This was going to be a long summer.

Chapter 3

"Rise and shine!" Shouted my father.

He opened the door to my bedroom, knocking loudly against the door frame. I was startled out of my sleep, jerking upwards with squinted eyes, holding my hand to my ear.

"Time for work." He said, leaning against the door frame, already fully dressed.

"What the hell dad?" I rubbed my eyes.

"Let's go. It's five o'clock. Breakfast is downstairs. Eat quick, it's going to be busy today."

I held up my hand, propping myself up with the other. "First of all, I had alarm set. Second, you need to knock before you come in."

"I did knock."

I huffed. "I said before you come in."

"You're my kid. I never had to knock when you were growing up."

"Well, things are different now." I pulled the covers up towards my chin. "You need to knock first, dad."

His mouth set in a hard line. Sometimes he forgot that the dynamic between us that he had been used to from my days before transitioning were non-existent now. He needed to respect my boundaries and privacy.

"Sorry… I'll be in the kitchen." He turned, leaving the doorway.

I huffed, tossing the covers aside as I got out of bed. I walked over to the door to close it. I rubbed my hands over my face, grunting with my back leaned against the door. I was in no mood to deal with my father or anyone for that matter. I hadn't even been in Brazil for twenty-four hours yet and was already done with it all. But sulking and arguing with him wasn't going to make the summer go by any faster. I pulled my scarf from my head and gathered my things to take a shower.

***

After my shower, I got dressed and met my father in the kitchen. He sat at the table, sipping coffee from his mug as he skimmed his newspaper reading whatever was trending on the local news front page. I dragged my feet over toward the table, knitting my eyebrows as I gazed over the plate of food my father had prepared for me.

"What's this?" I asked, sliding the rim of the plate around with my fingertips.

"Pao de queijo." My father replied. "Cheese rolls. They're good, I promise."

I took a seat across from him, unimpressed by his choice of breakfast cuisine. I picked up one of the puffy golden balls and bit into the chewy center.

"What do you think?" He asked as he watched me eat the pastry.

I just shrugged as I chewed. "It's not gross. But it ain't all that." I continued to eat the other rolls. "I'm guessing you don't have any grits around here."

"Nope."

His eyes drooped, he sat his cup on the table, sighing heavily. The phone rang, causing him to excuse himself from the table.

"Meet me in the car in five minutes." He grabbed the kitchen cordless phone to answer the call, heading out of the kitchen. And wear sneakers!" He called out before turning his attention to whoever was on the other end.

I reached into my crossbody purse and pulled out my HRT meds. Popping them in my mouth, I took a swig from the glass of orange juice he had set out for me. The realization that I was spending the next three months in an unfamiliar place with a man who struggled to understand me was setting in. I could feel my eyes glossing with tears as I held them back. The side effects of the hormone pills caused random emotional episodes that made my daily life as a trans teen even more complicated. But my sudden burst of sadness wasn't just the from the pills. Knowing that my father still held negative feelings towards me for being trans hurt more than anything. He'd never admit it, but he didn't have to. I could feel it, no matter how hard he tried to suppress them.

"Amari, let's go!" My father called out to me.

"I'm coming!" I yelled back. I wiped my eyes and stuffed the pill bottle back inside of my purse. I got up from the table, taking my plate and glass to the sink before hurrying outside to meet him at the car.

***

In a little under an hour later, we arrived at Coloma Village. A small agricultural community on the outskirts of Natal. I got out of the car, admiring the rural atmosphere of the village. Rows of green stretched acres across, with people in white shirts scattered around, all occupied with

various tasks. My father got out of the car and walked over to the passenger's side to stand next to me. "Beautiful isn't it?" He asked, watching me as I observed my surroundings. He guided me to a small building that resembled a church. "This is where my office is. Agriculture classes and volunteer training takes place here as well."

"I hope there's air conditioning at least." I whined, wiping the beading sweat from my forehead.

"Nope. But you'll be outside anyway." He said.

My eyes bulged. "Doing what? Don't I need to be trained or something?"

"No. Not right now anyway. It's harvest day. We need to get everything gathered for delivery this afternoon." He pointed in the direction of a stack of crates filled with little orange fruit. "You see those? Those are seriguelas. They need to be transported to the other side of the building for pick-up. I've got a meeting, but I'll have someone bring you a dolly."

He walked away, and I stood with my hand on my hip, looking over at the endless crates attacked around and on top of each other. With slumped shoulder's I walked over to the crates scrunching my face. A short, sweaty woman came back wheeling a dolly and sat it in front of me.

"Só três de cada vez." The woman said, holding up three fingers.

"Umm.. I don't speak Portuguese." I said to her.

"Três! Três!" The woman reiterated, still holding up three fingers. Before I could get another word out, the woman walked away.

I threw my head back, grunting loudly in frustration. The hot sun beamed down on my golden-brown skin that had already turned a shade darker, stinging the back of my neck. It was well over ninety degrees with a real feel of over a hundred. This humidity was nothing like what I was used to back home in Georgia. It hadn't even been twenty full minutes since I got out of the car and my shirt was already sticking to my back as sweat crept down my spine. I grabbed the first crate, placing it on the dolly. The quicker I could get this tiresome task done, the better.

Chapter 4

Drenched in sweat, I trudged towards the pick-up area with only half the crates finished. My arms were sore, my back ached, and I hadn't even seen my father since he left me to work like a slave. I didn't even work this hard in county lock up, which would have felt like heaven compared to the crappy day I was having. The wheels on the dolly began to wobble, the crates shifted side to side. I wrapped one arm around them to keep them secure as I rushed to drop them off. Suddenly, the wheels of the dolly gave out and the crates tumbled over, crashing on to the ground and taking me with them. Seriguelas spilled everywhere, my face flushed a crimson red.

"Dammit!" I shouted, kicking the dolly.

People standing nearby laughed, one of them was the short woman who brought me the dolly earlier. She shook her head, mumbling something to the others in Portuguese. I was fuming, I grabbed one of the crates that didn't break and aggressively tossed the fruit that I could gather up back inside. If this was my father's idea of a cruel joke, I was over it. I'd rather go back to the States than endure three months of this. As I hurried to gather up the fruit, a young man walked over to me. He kneeled and began to pick up the seriguelas.

"Olá." He said smiling at me. threading his hand through his long brunette hair and handing one of the fruits to me.

I snatched it from his hand, throwing it into the crate. "I don't speak Portuguese!" I scowled.

His expression hardened and his smile was gone. "I believe you're supposed to say thank you." He stood on his feet.

Slightly embarrassed, I didn't know what to say. I just continued to gather up the mess.

"Also, you should only stack three crates at a time." He said in a thick accent. I glared up at him. "That dolly is pretty old. It'll be easier for you." He peered down at me, the corners of his mouth raised as he smirked before walking away.

I then realized that the woman from earlier was trying to warn me about over stacking the crates. Plopping myself down on the ground, I angrily tossed one of the fruits across the dirt.

"What happened over here?" My father questioned as he came towards me, his face puckered.

I stood up, dusting off my shorts. "I can't do this!"

"It's not a big deal. We'll get this mess cleaned up and I'll grab another dolly."

"It's not about the stupid dolly!" I kicked one of the crates. "I can't do any of this! I know you want to punish me, I get it!"

"Punish you? Is that what you think?" He titled his head, crossing his arms.

"I want to go back home!"

He laughed. "You aren't going anywhere."

"I hate this!" I kicked the crate again, breaking it this time.

"Damarion Davis! You better get it together and fix that attitude!" He stood firmly, pointing at me. "You will not embarrass me in front of these people!"

I gasped, my lower lip trembling. I locked up with rage as my dead name slipped from his tongue. My father could see the anger radiate from me, the pain spilling from my eyes.

"I'm sorry… I didn't mean that…"

He tried to take it back, but the damage was done. I ran towards the building entrance, sadness tearing at my chest. He began to go after me but stopped himself. He knew it would just lead to another argument.

I swung the door open, heading straight down a narrow hall, unsure of where I was headed. I spotted two identical doors labeled in Portuguese. Assuming they were restrooms, I headed into the first one not caring if it was the female room or not. I barged in, running into one of the two stalls. It was a urinal, just my luck. I crouched on the floor and balled my eyes out. Dead naming was one of the worst things anyone could ever do to a trans person, and my father knew this. His slip up was just another heartbreaking reminder of how he truly felt about me. The restroom door cracked open. I blinked back my tears, wiping my face with the end of my shirt. The footsteps made their way towards the sink, there was a pause before the faucet turned on. I sat there in silence, waiting for them to hurry up and leave.

I could hear them grabbing paper towels, turning off the faucet. The person then turned and started walking towards my stall. Anxiety swirled around me as I drew myself backward. The person hunched down, reaching underneath my stall with paper towels in their hand. My chest rose and fell as I let out a sigh of relief. I reached for the paper towels taking them from his hands and wiping my face.

"Thanks." I said.

"Are you alright?" He asked from behind the door. I recognized that voice with the thick accent. It was the young man with the brunette hair, who helped me with the fruit.

"I'm fine." I sniffed, wiping the tears from my eyelids.

"You don't sound fine to me." He replied.

"It's really none of your businesses." I told him in crass tone.

"You don't have to be rude. You North Americans… sem maneiras."

I groaned as I got up, unlocking the stall and pushing the door open. He stood there, looking at me with hard, narrow eyes.

"You don't know a damn thing about me." I said. I tossed the balled-up paper towels to the floor, deliberately bumping his shoulder as I pushed past him to exit the restroom.

"Asshole!" I yelled out as I pushed through the door and stormed back down the hall. I came to a small empty room filled with boxes.

I eased my way inside, closing the door behind me. I locked the door to ensure I could sob in peace without anyone else invading my space. I squeezed past the boxes, sitting on the biggest one I saw. There was a knock on the door.

"Go away!" I buried my face in my palms, wishing whoever it was would just disappear.

"Amari, it's me." My father said softly from behind the door. "Amari, honey… please open the door." He jiggled the knob.

"I just want to be alone." I uttered. But I knew my father. He wouldn't leave until I opened that door.

"But I don't want my baby girl to be alone." He said. Warmth filled my chest. Baby girl. I hadn't heard him call me baby anything since I was nine years old. My father usually used gender neutral pronouns when speaking of me. In the eight years since my coming out, this was the first time he had ever called me that. I stood up, squeezing past the boxes again to unlock the door. I turned to go back to sit on the box as he opened the door. My eyes hung to the floor, he came over, taking a seat on the same box with his back to mine. We just sat there, silent. My father cleared his throat, and I felt him, peering back at me.

"Remember when you were a kid, and you would always ask to go the park with your little friend, the one with the runny nose?" I asked my father as he chuckled. "What was his name?"

"His name was Ronnie." I cracked a small smile as the memory came back.

"Yeah him. I always told you no, and you hated me for it every single time."

My smile faded. "Uh huh. How could I forget." I remembered fondly how strict he was when I was growing up. His authoritarian ways hadn't changed much over the years.

"I never let you go because I was too afraid that something bad would happen to you. He said. I felt the same way the day you told me you were a girl."

My stomach burned as I recalled that day. After my mother discovered the truth, I begged her not to tell him. I wanted it to come from me. I waited until he came home from deployment. He came by the house to see me as soon as his plane landed. When he arrived and walked through my mother's door I stood in front of him wearing a lavender romper from Goodwill, and a pair of bamboo earrings I stole from the Korean beauty supply. He looked dead at me, and I saw the excitement on his face dissipate into something unrecognizable. I'll never forget that day, because it was the last time, I saw him truly happy.

"When you came out, it was hard for me because I knew nothing would ever be the same again. For you, not for me. It was never about me. I've seen what happens out there, to girls like you. I didn't want you to end up dead in some hotel room. I couldn't go on if I lost you. When you went to jail, it destroyed me. I hated waking up every day for a year, knowing you were in there." My father wrapped his arm around my shoulder, pulling me closer as I laid my head under his arm. "I'm so sorry I called you out your name. I promise I'll never do that again. I love you Amari."

Tears bubbled at my eyelids, I wiped them from corner with thumb. "I love you too dad." This moment with my father, nestled under his arms filled me with joy. Truth be told, this was my main reason for agreeing to stay with him for the summer. I missed him so much.

"I always thought you tried to keep me from Ronnie because you knew I had a crush on him."

His nose crinkled. "No way, you could do better." We both laughed. He squeezed me tightly, and for the first time in a long time, I felt like my father loved me again.

Chapter 5

My second day in Coloma village was off to a much better start. I'd still be out in the heat unfortunately, but my father promised that I'd be spared of hard labor this time. He led me towards the entrance of the building, where a small group of people were standing around socializing. As we approached them, one face stood out amongst the rest.

"Good morning everyone!" My father greeted them. "I want you to meet someone. This is my daughter, Amari. She'll be joining us this summer."

They all gathered around to greet me, shaking my hand with faces full of smiles as my father introduced them one by one. All except for him.

"Amari, this is Gabriel Santos." My father introduced. "He's from one of the local non-profits that's partnered with the Corps."

The brunette boy that I had not one, but two unpleasant encounters with the day before stood in front of me. Forcing a half smile, he extended his hand out.

"Nice to meet you. Amari." He greeted me with an intrusive tone, as if knowing my name fascinated him. But not in a good way.

I took his hand, giving it a limp shake. "Hi." I muttered, avoiding his gaze as I let his hand go. A blonde girl with big green eyes eased past him, wearing a huge grin as she held her arm out to me.

"Hi Amari!" She exclaimed. "Glad to have you here! Marcus has told me so much about you!" Her accent was too familiar. A country girl.

"Amari this is Charlotte Cooper, from Texas. She works in the health sector. Where you'll be."

"Hey." I replied flatly. Her chipper personality was a bit off-putting, but I had to admit that it felt nice to have some familiarity here. All the others from the Corps that I had met so far were older, and/or from northeast states. But Charlotte was from the south like me, and closer to my age than the others.

"Come on girl!" Charlotte grabbed my arm and pulled me towards the door in a hurry. "Let's get to work!"

"I'll check in with you later honey!" My father called out to me as Charlotte dragged me inside.

"So, how are you liking Brazil so far?" She asked as she led me down the hall to a classroom.

"It's okay I guess." I said.

"I love it here! Some parts are kind of slummy. But my parents have money, so I don't have to live in the village like the other Peace Corp Volunteers. It gets tough here, but that's why the Corps is needed! To educate and improve!" Charlotte said, still wearing that wide grin.

We walked inside the classroom, where plastic crates sat on the desks and on the floor. Most filled with sanitary products, contraceptives, and stacks of brochures sat on the table near the chalkboard.

"Today you're going to help me separate and organize these items so they can be packed up. We send them to local schools, clinics, places that need them." Charlotte said as she grabbed a crate and handed it to me. "Take these to the table up front please."

She grabbed a crate and followed me to the front of the classroom. We placed the crates on the table, Charlotte walked towards an outlet where a small boom box sat on the floor. She plugged the cord into the socket and turned it on. "Oh my God! I love this song!" She began to sing along to Mariah Carey as Honey played mid-chorus. She was offbeat, but that didn't stop her from moving her little hips along to the beat while attempting a horrible Mariah impression. I laughed as I watched her dance while taking boxes of condoms out of the crate she handed me.

"You look and sound ridiculous. But it's cute though." I complimented, still laughing at her corny dance moves and lack of rhythm.

"I know I'm a rhythmically challenged white girl, but I get points for trying right?" She asked. We both laughed.

"Aren't you girls supposed to be working?" Asked a male voice.

I turned to see Gabriel walking inside the classroom holding unfolded boxes and masking tape. Not him again. I rolled my eyes. He approached Charlotte and I, dropping the boxes on the floor next to me.

"Aren't you supposed to be minding your own business?" Charlotte said as she walked over to the boom box to turn the music down. She walked over to Gabriel, throwing her arm around his neck and landing a kiss on his cheek. "Thanks for bringing these. You're sweet." She gave him another peck.

"No problem." Gabriel replied. His eyes roamed towards me, but I turned away and continued with my task.

"I've gotta go check in with Marcus to make sure the supply lists are updated. Charlotte looked my way. "Amari, I'll be right back."

She left the classroom, leaving me alone with him. He grabbed one of the boxes from the floor and began to fold it, using the tape to put it together. I walked over to one of the desks to retrieve another crate, trying my best to avoid eye contact on my way back to the table. The silence that filled the room made things awkward. All I could think about was him listening to me balling my eyes out in the men's restroom yesterday. How he called me a rude American, now I was mad all over again.

"I'm sorry about yesterday." Gabriel said.

"Huh?" I questioned. My brows drew together as I pretended I misheard him.

"Yesterday, when I called you a rude American. In the bathroom, remember?"

"Oh yeah." I continued to take the items out of the crate, completely apathetic towards Gabriel's apology. I refused to give him the satisfaction of knowing he had hurt my feelings.

"The girl's restroom is the one on the right by the way. In case you didn't know."

I halted again, running my tongue along my gums as I turned to him wearing a phony smirk. My eyes crinkling at the sides.

"Yes. I'm aware of that now. Maybe if there was a sign for me in English, I would've gone into the correct bathroom, instead of running into you."

This guy was really pushing it with me. With his heavy accent, I honestly couldn't tell if he was being serious or a smart-ass. I'm sure it was the latter. The corners of his mouth lifted, he sized me up with his hooded eyes.

"You should learn our language."

"And you should stop talking to me!" I yelled.

The door opened, and Charlotte walked back in. I quickly turned back around, attending to the crates as if the conversation between Gabriel and I had never happened.

"Gabriel, they need you out at the loading area." Charlotte told him as she grabbed another crate from one of the desks to bring it over.

"See you ladies later." He said, giving us a little salute before as he left the classroom.

"Bye!" Charlotte blew him a kiss, swooning over him with glinted eyes as she watched him leave.

She went back over to the radio to turn the music back up. A song by Alanis Morrisette was playing. She came back towards the table, humming along. I looked at her as she stood next to me, organizing the sex ed pamphlets into different stacks. Her hair had the perfect bounce to it, flowing just above her shoulders. Not a freckle or spot of blotchiness in sight. I could see why any guy would be crushing hard on a girl like her. The only guys who ever showed interest in me where street thugs who would've killed me once they clocked that I was trans. The creeps in prison didn't count. They were sexually starved and a 'tranny' as they called me, was the closest they would get to the touch of a woman. But girls like Charlotte had it sweet. She could probably get any guy she wanted. Must've been nice.

"I hope this doesn't offend you or anything, but your boyfriend is kind of an asshole." I said.

"My boyfriend? Are you talking about Gabriel?" She asked as she turned to me.

"Yeah."

"He's not my boyfriend. Well, not yet anyway." She swooped a lock of hair behind her ear. "We've had a thing for a while, but it's not serious yet." She nudged my elbow, giggling. "Why do you think he's an asshole? Did he say something to you?"

"Umm, no. It's nothing." I shook my head, not wanting to tell her about the bathroom situation or my embarrassing dolly mishap. "I think I'm getting him confused with someone else."

"Probably. Gabriel's such a sweetheart. That's why I like him." Her lashes fluttered as she got lost in a quick trance thinking about him. "Oh! Before I forget!" She snapped out of her daydream. "You should come to this beach party with me tomorrow night. It'll be fun. You can meet some more of my friends."

"That sounds fun, but I don't know…" This was only my third day and I was still getting used to the culture and people. Going to a party where I'd only know one person didn't feel safe. On the other hand, I had survived a year in jail. In the south. There wasn't much that could scare me at this point, even in a foreign country.

"Please!" She clasped her hands together, giving me puppy dog eyes with pouted lips. "There will be alcohol. Good stuff too."

"Okay. I'll go. But I have to check with my dad first."

"Awesome! You'll have a blast! I promise!" She hugged me with one arm.

Back home, I probably wouldn't have been friends with someone like Charlotte in a million years. But here, I felt like I had someone that could keep me sane for the time being. She was spunky and had alcohol. That was enough for me.

***

My father and I made our way towards the car as our day in Coloma had come to an end. The sudden urge to pee struck me, and I knew I couldn't hold it for that 45-minute drive back home.

"Dad, I'm gonna run to the bathroom before we leave." I told him.

"Make it quick." He said, getting in on the driver's side.

I jogged back to the building, heading to the restroom as quickly as I could. When I arrived at the restroom doors, I stopped. I peered at the paper sign taped to the center. For Girls. I looked over at the other door, where the same sign hung that read For Boys. I chuckled faintly, running my tongue along the inside of my cheek. A small burst of joy warmed me from within as a smile tugged at my lips. I opened the door and went inside.

Chapter 6

That night, Charlotte took us to Ponta Negra Beach, where locals had gathered for a bonfire party. We got out of Charlotte's car and headed towards the center, where a few dozen people, all drinking and fraternizing were surrounding the fire. Liquor bottles littered the sand, and the area reeked of marijuana.

"Olá bitches!" Charlotte screamed, holding up two cases of beer as we approached a girl and two guys sitting in lawn chairs a few feet away from the crowd.

"It's about time you showed up." The girl said to Charlotte, taking one of the beer cases from her hand. She looked up at me. *"Ela é linda.* Whose your friend?" She asked, blowing smoke from her nose.

"This is Amari. She works with me in Coloma." Charlotte replied. "Amari these are my friends Natalia and Ramon."

"You smoke?" Ramon asked. Reaching his hand out to hand me a joint.

"No, I'm good actually." I waved it off. "I'll take some of whatever you're drinking though."

He kneeled to pick up an unlabeled bottle of brown liquor. Handing it to me. I popped open the top and chugged it down to the center. Charlotte's eyes grew wide.

"Damn girl! Save some for the rest of us!" She giggled, taking the joint from Ramon and inhaling before passing it to Natalia. I passed the bottle back to Ramon and grabbed a beer from the case.

"North American girls who like to party. Ramon Said. "My favorite." He smirked, chugging from the liquor bottle I had just drank from.

"Speaking of party, why are we still over here? Let's go where all the action is!" Charlotte said as she grabbed my arm and pulled me towards the fire.

Samba music blasted from a huge boom box as people danced around the bonfire, drunk and high out of their minds. Charlotte and I squeezed passed a couple making out, their sweaty bodies bumping against ours. I wasn't the partying type, and the summer heat mixed with the flames from the fire made me uncomfortable with so many people confined to one space. I could see that Charlotte was already buzzed, gyrating around as she clung to Ramon who was also drunk.

Once I noticed that Charlotte was distracted, I eased my way out of the crowd, trying to get as far away from that inferno of sweaty intoxicated bodies as I could. The tide was coming in, so I decided to walk along the beach just to take in the scenery. I walked over to a set of rocks, taking a seat on top of one of them. Just watching the waves crash and stars that lit the dark night sky. I couldn't remember the last time I felt this relaxed and composed.

"Can I sit? Or will you scream at me?" A male voice called from behind me.

My heart jumped as I turned to see who the hell was behind me. I held my hand against my chest, sighing in relief when I saw a familiar face. "Jesus, you nearly gave me a heart attack."

"I didn't mean to scare you. Sorry." Gabriel stood peering down at me, holding a small cup of liquor.

I held the sides of my arms, exhaling through my nose with pressed lips as I observed him standing there. Waiting for an invitation to sit next to me. "You can sit. I don't mind."

He walked around and sat on the rock next to me. He sipped from his cup, facing forward and watching the waves with me. Our last few encounters hadn't been pleasant, so I wasn't sure why he had even bothered to come over here. I suddenly remembered about the signs on the restroom doors.

"Thanks for the signs on the bathroom doors."

"I have no idea what you're talking about." He said in a snarky tone. I squinted at him. He turned to me, expressionless at first. Then his expression softened. A smile danced on his soft lips. I had never been this close to him before. His eyes were a soft mix of honey and sage. I hadn't noticed until this moment, as he sat inches away from me with his smooth hair pulled back into a bun.

"You're welcome." He said.

I smiled, looking down at the sand under me and I fiddled with my thumbs.

"I really appreciate that." A feeling of guilt overcame me. Charlotte was right. Gabriel was a sweetheart, and I hadn't been nice at all.

"I'm sorry. I was a bit of a bitch to you yesterday."

"And the day before."

I scoffed, nudging his arm. "Look, I'm trying to apologize. Don't ruin it."

"I'm kidding." He laughed. "No really, it's fine. I know what it's like being new in an unfamiliar place." He took a sip from his cup. "My father was Italian. I was born here, but we lived in Italy for a year when I was seven. It sucked. I couldn't speak Italian and I was a little too brown to fit in with the other kids."

"Maybe you should've learned the language." I mocked jokingly.

"Wow. You've got jokes now? I guess I deserved that."

"Mm hmm." I slithered a flat smirk through crooked lips.

He laughed, surveying me with his deep-set eyes. "I can teach you, if you want. Or... I could keep making signs in English and just hang them up everywhere. Whichever you'd like."

A flush crept up my face, I giggled. "That actually sounds a lot easier."

"I'll keep my pen handy then." He grinned. There was that smile again.

I noticed someone stumbling towards us from the corner of my eye. I turned and it was Charlotte, lit out of her mind.

"What are you guys doing way over here?" She asked through her slurred speech. "Gabriel! Why didn't you tell me you were here?" She approached him, leaning down and wrapping her arms around him from behind and resting her head on his shoulder.

"You seemed like you were having so much fun already." He said sarcastically.

Charlotte's fluffy waves draped over her crimson face as she clung on to Gabriel, tumbling sideways, nearly pulling him towards the sand with her as she fell over.

"Oh my gosh! Are you okay?" I got up, kneeling beside her. Gabriel pulled up one of her eyelids, his brows raised with concern.

"Wow. Again?" He pinched the bridge of his nose, pulling her up by her arms and holding her against him as she tried to stand on her feet.

"What's wrong? Is she okay?" I asked, assisting him in keeping her steady.

"She's high, and it's not marijuana. Who knows what kind of pills her friends gave her this time. We should get her out of here before she kills herself."

This Time? My mouth fell open, I surveyed Charlotte as Gabriel led us to his car. Her pupils were abnormally enlarged, and her cheeks and forehead were flushed red. She told me she liked to drink, and smoke weed occasionally, but I never pegged her as a pill popper. We reached his ash colored pick-up truck, he opened the front seat door hoisting Charlotte up and sliding her in the middle of the seat.

I hung my head back. "Crap."

"What's wrong?" Gabriel asked me.

"Charlotte was my ride home."

"That's alright. Now I'm your ride. Get in." He inclined his head, gesturing for me to get in. "I live closer, so we'll take Charlotte to my place then I'll take you home. Is that okay?"

I nodded yes, pulling myself up, sliding in on the driver's side and scooting Charlotte over to make room for Gabriel in the driver's seat. He got in, starting the engine and driving away from the pier as we headed to his house.

Chapter 7

We arrived at Gabriel's home fifteen minutes later. A one-story colonial style house with indigo blue shutters and a Spanish tiled roof. It resembled my dad's home, which had a similar exterior with the titled roof. Gabriel parked, getting out on his side and coming around to the passenger side where Charlotte was sitting. She had fallen asleep during the drive, slouched over with her head on my shoulder. Gabriel opened the door, holding Charlotte and placing her arm over his shoulder as he led her out of the truck, half-awake and disoriented. I followed behind, holding on to Charlotte's other arm. He pulled out his keys as we approached his door. Once we were inside he led us towards a brown sofa.

"Vovó, você está acordado?" Gabriel called out to someone as we placed Charlotte across the sofa. I could hear a woman mumbling in Portuguese from another room.

"Sim, sim, o que é isso Gabriel?" She said in a weary tone. A short woman in a nightgown came slowly plodding into the living room, rubbing her eyes. They widened once she saw me and Charlotte. "Oh, hello!" She greeted with a smile.

"Amari, this is my grandmother, Marcia." Gabriel said.

"Nice to meet you." I waved, grinning with pressed lips.

"Grandma, this is Amari. She works with Charlotte and me in the village. Marcus' daughter."

"Another North American girl. She said smiling. "Lovely to meet you too, Amari." Marcia walked towards me, extending her arms out for a hug. "Don't be shy, I don't bite." Her arura was welcoming. I embraced her hug. She looked over at Charlotte, passed out on her sofa. "Again? *Patética.*" Said Marcia as she wrinkled her nose is disgust. "That girl is no good for you Gabriel. No good." She waggled her finger.

"Grandma, not now." Gabriel huffed, his forehead creased.

"What? It's true. She's always high, drunk, something. You can do better. Much better." Marcia rolled her eyes. She faced me, grinning and wrapping her frail hand around my arm. "Amari, such a gorgeous young woman. Don't you think so *meu neto*?" She pinched my cheek and looked at Gabriel.

"Yes, I do." He replied. Wearing a lopsided grin, he shoved his hands into his pockets. Heat crept on to my cheeks. We shared a glance as I held my arms. A smile tugged at my lips. "I'm gonna grab a blanket for Charlotte. I'll be right back." Gabriel left the living room. I stood there, drawing my lower lip between my teeth. Unsure of how to react towards Gabriel's compliment.

"So, Amari, where are you from?" Marcia asked.

"Georgia. It's in the south." I told her.

"Georgia huh? That sounds lovely. I remember my days in the states. I lived in New York for a year. But that was ages ago." Her eyes hung to the floor, I could tell that she was having a moment of reminiscing about that time.

"Did you like it?" I asked.

"I loved it. Would've stayed if I could. But... circumstances brought me back here." She walked over to a nearby table and picked up a framed photo. "This was me in '53. Taken in central park. I was 23 years old. That's me on the left."

She handed me the faded photo. In the picture was her and another woman, sitting on a park bench. The other woman had bright red hair, that stood out even in the aged photograph. Marcia rested her head on the woman's shoulder, with her leg crossed. They looked happy, in an intimate way. I didn't want to make any assumptions, but I knew a couple when I saw one.

"She's pretty." I handed her back the photo.

"Yes, she was. We had some good times together back then, Rose and I." Her smile faded. Her thumbs brushed the edge of the frame as a wave of sadness overcame her. "Anyways, enough about me!" She placed the photo back on the table. "What brings you to Brazil?" She asked excitedly, patting my back.

"Just spending time with my dad. It's just for the summer."

"Well I hope your summer in Natal is amazing! There is so much to see and do!" She said.

"Hopefully. But we'll see." I replied, shrugging my shoulders.

Gabriel came from back to the living room holding a light blue kitted blanket. He kneeled next to Charlotte, gently draping the blanket over her.

"She's staying here for the night. I'll take her to get her car from the pier in the morning."

"Yeah, yeah. Sure." Marcia waved, dismissively.

"I'm gonna take Amari home. I'll be back." Gabriel told her. He stood up, taking his keys from his pocket. "You ready?"

"Yeah." I answered, avoiding his gaze.

"It really was a pleasure to meet you, young lady. Come by again anytime!" She leaned over to hug me again.

Gabriel and I made our way towards the door, I turned to wave goodbye to Marcia as we went outside.

"I hope my grandmother didn't bother you too much. She's very affectionate with everyone." Gabriel said, opening the passenger door to his truck as we approached.

"No, it's fine. She's very sweet." I said as I climbed inside.

"Good. I wouldn't want her scaring off the new girl." He grinned, closing the door as he made his way over to the driver's side.

"Scaring me off?" My brows snapped together. "It'll take a lot more than a friendly old lady to scare me off."

"Is that right?" He asked, wearing a smirk as he got inside. "Well I'm glad. She seems to like you a lot. Grandma has a soft spot for U.S. girls. Except for Charlotte of course."

"Yeah, I noticed.". We both laughed as he started the engine and drove away.

***

I sat with my hands in my lap, tapping my fingers against my knees as we cruised down the dark, dim lit streets. I kept my head facing out of the window, turning occasionally to steal a glance while he focused on the road. When I wasn't looking, I could see him peering over at me from the corner of my eye.

"So, what's the deal with you and Charlotte anyway?" I asked Gabriel, still looking out of the window.

"Me and Charlotte? What do you mean?"

I turned to face him. "Don't play dumb. You know what I mean."

He hunched his right shoulder, trying to hide his sly grin. "I'm not playing. I'm just asking you to clarify."

"She likes you. A lot. I've seen you two kiss."

"You've seen her kiss me." He held up a finger in protest. "Not the other way around."

I rolled my eyes. "So? What's the difference?"

"The difference is, she likes me. I never said the feeling was mutual. You assumed it was."

"I'm not assuming anything. Just asking."

"Why are you asking?"

My jaw went slack. "Because I felt like it." I scoffed, folding my arms. We approached a stoplight, and the tension in the truck seemed to increase as we both sat in silence. My dad's house was fifteen minutes from Gabriel's, yet this ride felt like it was taking forever. That's when I heard the engine shut off, and Gabriel removed his keys from the ignition.

"Umm… what are you doing?" My eyes perked up. "Why are we stopping? Take me home. Now!"

"Amari, would you like to go out with me?" He asked.

We stared at one another, the expression on my face softened. "Excuse me?"

"Would you, Amari… like to go on a date. With me?"

"I hardly even know you."

"Let's get to know each other then."

"Why?" I questioned. "So you can sweet talk me into sleeping with you? I'm not that kind of American girl, honey."

He chuckled faintly, running his thumb across his chin. "You could've just said no."

"I never said no. I'm just keeping it real with you."

"Keeping it real? What does that mean?" He asked.

"It means that I'm just letting you know that I don't have time for games. I don't like being taken advantage of, and quite frankly it wouldn't be a good idea on your part."

He surveyed my eyes and could tell that I was serious. "That's not my intention, at all. I'm sorry if you got that impression." He put the keys back in the ignition and started the engine. "Let's go somewhere right now."

My brows rose with uncertainty. "Right now?" I looked at my watch. It was already past midnight.

"Yes. Right now. Wherever you want to go."

I sat there with my shoulders slumped. "I don't even know where anything is. Besides, it's late. It's hot as hell, and I'm thirsty."

"I know a place, not too far from here that makes really good *Vitamina de abacate*."

"Vitamina de what?" I asked, confused as hell.

He laughed. "Vi-ta-mi-na-de aba-cate." He enunciated slowly with curved lips. "It's a fruit smoothie."

"A smoothie actually sounds really good."

"So, that's a yes?" He confirmed, with his hands pressed firmly on the steering wheel.

I pursed my lips, trying to hide a smile that attempted to slip through. "Yes."

He smiled as we pulled away from the intersection. Heading to what would technically be, my very first date.

Chapter 8

He took me to a little café, located near the pier. We went inside, alcohol and unfamiliar exotic spices tinged my nostrils. Gabriel led us to the bar, greeting the woman standing behind the counter.

"Ola!" He waved as we took a seat on the wooden stools.

"Ola Gabriel! What can I do for you?" She asked, leaning forward with her arms stretched.

"Vitamina de abacate. Two please." He said, holding up two fingers.

The woman looked at me, raising an eyebrow. She slightly pursed her lips. "Who is this querida? New girlfriend huh?" She winked at me, smiling.

"This is Amari." He turned to me, the corners of his lips rose. "She's a friend."

"Well two Vitamina's for you and your friend, coming right up." She walked away to go make our drinks. I sat with my elbows on the counter, my eyes darting everywhere but at Gabriel. Who couldn't seem to keep his eyes off of me.

"Thank you for coming here with me." He said softly.

"Thank you for asking." I replied, I pushed a lock of hair behind my ear, meeting his eyes again.

The woman came back with two plastic cups of a thick green liquid. I swirled the straw around, my forehead creased.

"What kind of fruit is this?" I asked.

"It's avocado, sugar and milk. We use avocado as a fruit here." Gabriel said, sipping from his straw.

"That sounds gross." My upper lip curled, my thirst slowly faded at the sight of my unappealing drink.

"Try it. You'll like it. I promise."

I placed my lips over the straw, taking a small sip. My brows shot up as the chill of sweet flavors hit my tongue. "You were right! I do like it!" I took another, longer sip. "I've never had sweet avocado before."

"Told you it was amazing. You're welcome." He simpered, looking pleased with himself.

He reached behind his head, pulling off the small rubber band that held his oily brunette hair together in a messy bun. He threaded his hands through his hair, pushing it away from his face.

I didn't blame Charlotte for having such a huge crush on him. Gabriel was honestly, one of the most beautiful boys I had ever seen. Charlotte. Guilt pinched the pit of my stomach as I thought about her. Even though we had only known each other for less than two days, I considered her a friend. Some friend I was, being here on a date with the guy she liked. Knowing she was passed out on his couch at this very moment, made it even worse.

"I do feel kind of bad, being here." I admitted.

"Why?" His eyelids drooped. "Don't tell me it's because of Charlotte. Do you know what would've happened if we hadn't taken Charlotte back to my house?" He asked. "She would've left with Ramon. Like she always does."

My eyes widened, I nearly spit out my smoothie. "Seriously?"

"There is a reason me and Charlotte aren't together. Well, that and the fact that she's not really my type anyway."

"Oh really? What's your type?" I questioned in a cheeky manner.

"Girls who shove me in restrooms."

We both went silent, breaking the awkward moment with a laugh. "I didn't shove you. I bumped you." I said, swinging my hair behind my shoulder. "Well you were in my way."

I batted my lashes, cracking a smile. The memory of that day Gabriel walked in on me crying in the restroom, flooded back to the front of my mind. Reality began to set in as my smile faded. Gabriel could tell that my mood had shifted. He placed his hand on my shoulder.

"Hey, are you alright?" He asked, with genuine concern in his eyes. "Do you wanna talk about about it?"

I nodded, pushing my drink away. "It's pretty late. I think I should go."

"Sure. Let's get you home." He said without hesitation. We got up from our seats, and headed back to his truck.

***

After our short but enjoyable little date, we had finally arrived at my dad's house. Gabriel parked his truck, reached over into his glove compartment. He pulled out a piece of paper, closing the compartment back and grabbing a pen that sat on his dashboard. I peeked over as he wrote something down on the paper. He tossed the pen back on the dashboard and handed me the paper.

"What's this?" I asked as I began to unfold it. There was a number written on it.

"It's my phone number." He said. "If you ever wanna talk."

I folded the paper, sticking it in the pocket of my jeans as we both got out, heading to the font door.

"I enjoyed spending time with you, even though it was cut short." He said.

"So did I." I replied, biting my bottom lip. I reached into my purse to grab to my key.

"So, I'll see you at the village tomorrow?"

There was a longing in his voice I hadn't heard before. When I looked into his eyes, they held a tender expression. The way he looked at me made my skin prickle. No guy had ever made me feel like this before. before.

"Yeah, of course, I'll be there," I replied. I unlocked the door and eased my way inside. "Good night Gabriel."

"Good night, Amari,"

I closed the door gently, trying not to wake my father. I headed to my room quietly, tossing my purse on my bed and heading straight to the bathroom. I got undressed, removing the duct tape that hid the worst part of me. The flesh between my legs that was a constant reminder of my real imprisonment. My body. I grabbed my meds from the cabinet, taking my nightly dose of HRT before I settled for bed. I grabbed my pants from the floor, reaching into the pocket and retrieving the paper Gabriel gave me. I was seconds away from tossing it into the trash bin beneath the sink. But I couldn't.

Dealing with guys back home was easier. They usually just wanted sex, which made rejecting them a simple task. But Gabriel was different. He had taken me on a real date. Like how guys treat girls in movies. Everything about this was foreign to me, and scary as hell. But the longer I stood there with the paper in my hands, the more I wanted to see him again. I clenched the paper in the palm of my hands, leaving my bathroom to get in bed. I placed the paper on the nightstand, putting on my night gown and wrapping my hair up before climbing in bed. An hour had passed, and I couldn't get to sleep. My hormone meds usually helped me sleep, but not tonight. I tossed and turned repeatedly, becoming frustrated with every passing minute I remained awake. At this point, I needed a distraction. I thought about Gabriel, wondering if he'd answer if I called. It was worth a try.

I turned over, grabbing the paper with his number and unfolding it. I reached for my cordless phone that sat on the charger next to it. I dialed his number, anxiety swirled around in my stomach as I waited for him to answer.

"Ola" He greeted from the opposite end.

"Hi, it's me. Amari." I sat up, pressing the phone against my ear. I hope it's not a bad time to be calling. I know it's late."

"No, no it's fine. I'm glad you called. I wasn't sleeping anyway."

"I felt bad about our date ending so suddenly. Figured I'd give you call, if you wanted to talk."

"Don't feel bad. It's okay. We can talk."

I propped myself up with one elbow. "So… what's your story anyway?"

"My story?"

"Like, what's your deal? Why did you really ask me out?"

"Well, I think you're hot. Even though you wanted to kill me when we first met."

I blushed. "I really am sorry about that. I was just dealing with a lot. With my dad. It wasn't you."

"I could tell. I saw you two arguing outside. I get it. I didn't have the best relationship with my father either. We used to argue a lot, before he died."

"How did he die?"

"He was sick. He died when I was fifteen. Six months before my mother passed away. She was sick too."

"Oh my God, I'm so sorry." I felt like crap for even asking.

"It's alright. I still have my grandma. She's as healthy as it gets. I'm thankful for that. So, enough about me. What about yourself?"

"Me? My life isn't that interesting."

"I don't believe you."

"It's true."

"Something brought you here to Brazil. I've known your dad for two years, but he never mentioned having a daughter until a few weeks ago when he told us you'd be coming."

A weight settled on my heart. "Really?" I didn't expect him to brag about me to the world, but hearing that he never even mentioned me, hurt.

"Yeah. That's why I assumed you two weren't close."

"We used to be. When I was little. But things changed."

"What kind of things?"

I winced, tightening my grip on the phone. "Things I don't really want to talk about."

"I understand. A woman's heart is a deep ocean of secrets."

"You stole that line from Titanic!" I laughed.

"You caught me. It's one of my favorite American films. My grandma's too."

"Same! My mom and I went to see it in theatres right before my…" I paused before I said too much.

"Before your what?" He asked, eager to hear the rest.

"If I tell you something, can you keep it between us?"

"Of course. What is it?"

I drew in a long breath, hesitant to open up to him. "I spent a year in jail. I just got out six months ago. Things were rough back home, so my mom sent me here to live with my dad and work for the summer. They said the experience would be good for me. Whatever that means." I took in a deep breath. "So, that's why I'm here. That's also probably why my dad never really mentioned me before. I'm not exactly a kid worth bragging about."

"Wow." He went silent.

This didn't feel good. There was no way he'd still like me after finding out I was a criminal. In a way, I hoped he wouldn't. It would've made things easier on my behalf. That was just the tip of the iceberg of what I was hiding from him.

"Are you going to tell me what you did?" He asked eagerly. "Did you rob a bank? Steal a car? Kill someone?"

"No, nothing like that." I giggled. "I stole a few credit cards."

"Just a few?"

"Okay a lot of credit cards." I rolled my eyes. "But I needed the money."

Gabriel sucked his teeth. "Amateur."

"Excuse me? That's a federal crime! Amateur my ass!"

"My dad was in the Italian mob. A real criminal."

My mouth fell open. "Oh damn! That's wild!"

"Tell me about it. It's one of the reasons me and him never got along. The lifestyle he lived put my mother through hell. He taught me a few things, how to pick pockets, scam tourists. But I haven't done those things since I was like fourteen."

I was speechless. Gabriel seemed like the type of guy that helped old ladies across the street. Not the type to rob them once they got across.

"So, you're not so innocent after all."

"Nope. I have a past, just like you." He said.

Gabriel and I were more alike than I ever would have thought. I felt like he understood me. I could tell him sensitive things about myself. Things that other people frowned upon me for. But he didn't judge. He empathized.

"Can I ask you something?" He asked.

"Sure, go ahead."

"Will you go on another date with me?"

I paused, hesitating to answer. "Maybe."

"How can I convince that maybe to turn into a yes?"

"You don't have to do anything. I just need to think about it."

"I'll keep my fingers crossed." He said in a hopeful tone.

"You do that. I'm gonna try and get some sleep. I'll see you in a few hours."

"Sleep well beautiful. Thanks for calling me."

"Bye." I hung up, placing the phone back on its charger. That talk with Gabriel had eased my mood, making it easier for me to fall asleep. I smiled, thinking about how a dolly full of fruit had led up to this. I had no idea what I was getting myself into with this boy. But I was willing to test the waters. Even if it was just for a little while.

Chapter 9

I eased my way into the room where Charlotte was having one of her classes on HIV/AIDS prevention. The room was full of young teenage girls, some even expecting mothers and as young as twelve. They were watching a video on the importance of getting tested. My father told me before we arrived that today was one of their monthly HIV testing days. I had gotten tested right after I was released from jail. Thankfully, my results came back negative. Contracting the virus was one of my biggest fears while I was locked up. Knowing my status was a huge relief and was one less thing I had to worry about as I started my new life on the outside. Although I hadn't been with anyone since jail, my father urged me to get tested again anyway. I figured there was no harm in doing it again, just so he'd stop asking.

Charlotte saw me coming in, waving excitedly as I took a seat in the back. I waved back, surveying the room for Gabriel. I didn't see him, so I figured my dad had him doing something else. Charlotte got up from her desk, making her way towards the back to sit next to me.

"Oh my gosh! Last night must've been crazy!"

She exclaimed in a stage whisper. "I don't even remember anything. Do you?"

You were pretty wasted." I said.

"All I remember is dancing by the fire. Next thing I know, I woke up on Gabriel's sofa this morning with a dry mouth and a headache." She chuckled. "He told me that he took you home when we left the party. I thanked him for looking out for you."

It was obvious that Gabriel didn't tell her about our little date. I figured he wouldn't. It wasn't any of her business anyway.

"Yeah, I got home okay."

"Thank God. Your father would kill me if anything happened to you. Sorry about that. We'll have a designated driver next time." She grinned, leaning in and hugging me with one arm. "Oh! Speaking of next time, this weekend we're all going zip lining on Fernando de Noronha. It's a little island off the coast of here. Not too far. You're going."

I scrunched up my face. "Hold up, wait. You're doing what and where now?"

"Zip lining. You've never done it before?" She asked with furrowed brows.

I nodded no.

"Well even more reason for you to come!"

This girl was yet again, trying to drag me on some wild outing with strangers. "Will Gabriel be there?" I asked.

"Yeah." She squinted at me slightly. "Why are you so curious?" She questioned.

I went poker-faced and twisted my hair around my finger. "No reason. Just a question."

Charlotte's eyes still dug into me. "Do you like him or something?"

My eyes shot up. "No! Not at all!" I let out a bitter laugh.

The corners of her mouth quirked up. "I'm kidding!" She slapped my shoulder. "You should've seen your face!" She giggled. "I'm just teasing you. Besides, I don't think Gabriel likes Black girls." She tilted her head as she looked heavenward, then back at me. "No offense of course!"

Wow. I pressed my lips together, staring at her with a blank expression. I know her intentions weren't to be rude, but the ignorance behind her remark still rubbed me the wrong way. Not only that, but she was wrong about Gabriel. I guess she didn't know her crush as well as she thought she did. The satisfaction I got from knowing that, caused a smile to slip through my lips.

"No offense taken girl." I gave her a phony grin.

The video ended, Charlotte got up and headed towards the front of the class. She began to speak in their native language, before dismissing them to leave. They got up from their seats and headed out of the room, Charlotte followed behind.

"You're getting tested today too, right?" She asked as I got up from my seat. "Even if you know you're clean, the volunteers still get tested once a month. We lead by example, and it encourages the locals who participate in the health program to take their sexual health seriously."

"Yeah of course." I said, following her out of the room with the others. We headed down the hall, and outside to the mobile testing station. I noticed Gabriel heading inside of the building. "I gotta use the restroom. I'll be right back." I told Charlotte. She nodded, and I made my way back inside the building to catch up with Gabriel. He was carrying a small package, headed down the hall.

"Hey!" I called out to him, jogging in his direction.

He turned around. his face lit up with a smile as I approached him. "Hey! I was hoping I'd see you today!"

"I just wanted to say hi." I stood with one hand on my hip. "What are you up to?"

"Just getting some packages sorted in the supplies room. What about you?" He asked.

"Charlotte and I are about to get tested out at the mobile station. Have you gotten yours done already?" I asked.

"Actually no. I've had it done recently, so I don't need it."

"Oh, cool." I fiddled with my hoop earring, looking down at the floor. This was awkward. "So, Charlotte invited me to go zip lining this weekend. She said you're going too."

"I told her I might. But if you're going, then I'll go." He said.

"I've gotta ask my dad first. But he should be cool about it."

"I hope so. It's pretty fun. You'll have a good time. Well, I've got work to do. I'll see you later?"

"Sure." I turned to head back outside.

"Amari, wait…" He called out to me. I turned to see what he wanted. "About that second date…"

The corners of my eyes crinkled. "I'm still thinking." I continued on my way, cracking a smile.

***

That night at dinner, my father and I watched The Lost World and enjoyed take out from a Mediterranean Resturant that he got me hooked on. I wasn't a fan of the food in South America, but this place made the tastiest gyros I had ever had. It felt good to have this quality time with my father again, just like old times when I was little. He was in one of his relaxed moods, which was the perfect time to bring up the zip lining trip.

"Charlotte invited me to go zip lining." I tossed out casually between bites of my food.

"Mm Hmm…" He uttered, too immersed in the movie to pay my comment any mind.

"Zip lining. It's on some island near here. Fernando-something. Can I go?"

He slipped me a curious glance. Fernando de Noronha? I've been there. It's a beautiful place." He grabbed a napkin, wiping his mouth. "Who else is going?"

"Umm… Charlotte and a few of her friends." I narrowed my eyes. "Why do you ask?" He didn't seem this concerned about the party I went to.

"I'm your father. I have a right to know who you're hanging out with."

I rolled my eyes. "Just a few people she knows. I met them at the party. They're cool peeps, no need to worry dad."

"Okay, just asking." He focused his attention back to the TV. "Who were you on the phone with last night?" His eyes circled back to me.

An unsettling feeling spiraled through me. I didn't think he was awake when I came home. "Nobody. I lied. "I mean, Charlotte. I was talking to Charlotte."

"Charlotte huh?" He questioned, wincing at me. He knew I was full of shit. But he had no proof to call me out on it. A smirk appeared on his face, he picked up his fork, taking another bite of his food. "Well, tell Charlotte that I don't allow any phone calls after midnight." He gave me a stern look. "And yes, you can go."

"Thank you daddy!" I reached over, wrapping my arms around him and squeezing him tightly. While I was glad that he was letting me go, I was a bit more to apprehensive about getting too close to Gabriel now. My father caught on to things a little too quickly, and I wasn't ready to tell him about Gabriel just yet. I wasn't even sure if there was anything to tell.

Chapter 10

"Amari, let's get going!" Charlotte yelled from my living room.

"Girl, don't you rush me!" I yelled back, adjusting my 12-inch clip on ponytail in my mirror. I ran my fingers through the synthetic hair piece, making sure it was slick and tangle-free. I had never done any nature-related activities like zip lining before, so I wasn't sure what to wear. I played it safe and decided on a simple spaghetti strap crop top and tan cargo shorts. I'd be comfortable and still look cute. I grabbed my backpack and headed out to the living room.

"Look at you, hottie!" Charlotte complimented with a finger snap.

"It's what I do best." I grinned, swaying my ponytail.

"Alright now. Don't have too much fun." My father said, moving in for a hug. "Be safe you two. Call me when you're near a phone, okay?"

"Yeah I will." I reassured him, wrapping my arms around him.

Charlotte and I headed out, ready to meet up with the others at the harbor.

***

We arrived at Negra harbor where Ramon, Natalia, and Gabriel were boarding a small powerboat. Charlotte and I grabbed our bags and met them at the dock. Gabriel waved as soon as he spotted us, leaning against the edge of the boat. His eyes focused on me, I waved back with a smile. My backpack hanging from one shoulder.

"It's about time!" Natalia whined playfully, approaching us as her and Charlotte greeted each other with soft cheek kisses. She leaned in towards me, giving me the same customary greeting.

"Good to see you again." I said, returning the gesture.

"Are we all good to go?" Charlotte asked, scurrying towards the guys and tossing her bag over and inside the boat.

Ramon reached out to help her inside, wrapping his arms around her waist and planting a kiss on her cheek. She giggled, playfully shoving him away. The more I saw them interact, the less I cared about Charlotte's so-called feelings for Gabriel. She obviously didn't like him that much, so hiding any interest I had in him to spare her feelings felt pointless.

Gabriel walked towards me as I reached the boat, taking my bag and extending his hand to me. "Welcome aboard." He grinned, taking my hand and hoisting me up inside the boat.

He climbed in behind me, I took a seat in the empty spot next to Natalia as Ramon started the motor and took us on our way.

"I'm glad you came." Gabriel said to me, sitting by my side.

"I'm glad you came too." I smiled, holding my arms together and peering out at the crisp blue water as we headed to the island of Fernando de Noronha.

***

Fernando de Noronha was unlike anything I had ever seen before. The water surrounding the island was an electric blue, I could see the coral reefs so clearly. We passed through a school of barracudas as we reached the land, with turtles inching at the edge of the water. My eyes gleamed at the breathtaking sight of it all. Ramon docked the boat and we all grabbed our things and headed on to the island.

"Beautiful, isn't it?" Gabriel asked, marveling at the sight too as he stood next to me.

"I've never seen anything like it." I surveyed my surroundings in awe.

"You haven't seen anything yet!" Charlotte exclaimed as we began our trek to the zip lining site.

Tucked beneath jagged cliffs and caves lurked exquisite white sand beaches. The rugged landscape of rocks and caves was like a page straight out of a National Geographic magazine. We hiked uphill, coming to a 250 ft tall lighthouse. There was a latter attached to the side of the narrow building going all the way up. They said that the entrance to the lighthouse was locked, so climbing the ladder was our only way to the top. I looked up, shading my eyes from the glaring sun. I could see the black rope that stretched far across to another part of the island.

My stomach rumbled. I was beginning to rethink this. I wasn't afraid of heights, but this was more extreme than I had imagined. Everyone dug into their bags, getting their supplies ready and putting on their gear. Charlotte brought an extra helmet and harness for me. I stood there struggling to figure out the harness. I looked around at the others who had put theirs on with a breeze.

"Let me help you." Gabriel offered, grabbing and unstrapping my harness. "This part goes under your legs. Then the other, around your waist. Like this." He moved the straps around my mid-section, positioning them perfectly in place.

"Thanks for helping." I said, putting on my helmet next.

He reached for the straps, snapping the clamp together under my chin. "Anytime." His soft smirk had suddenly eased the bitter feeling in my stomach.

"Can we go now?" Charlotte said smugly, glancing at Gabriel and I before heading up the ladder first. Natalia and Ramon followed behind her.

"After you." Gabriel insisted.

I headed up the ladder behind Natalia, clenching the handles firmly and trying not to look down.

"How long does it take to get to the top?" I asked, keeping my eyes focused on the bars.

"About twenty minutes. Fifteen if you're fast." Natalia said from above.

Oh God. I needed a distraction if I was going to make it to the top of this tower in one peace. Singing was the only thing I could think of to pass the time. I hummed Use Your Heart by SWV under my breath as I continued up. It helped ease my anxiety and as I peered above, it seemed like we were getting closer. I hummed two more songs to myself, and before I knew it, we had finally reached the roof.

My jaw hung open as I gazed out at the island landscape from twenty-three stories high. Charlotte wasted no time, using the lanyard to connect her trolley to her harness.

"You're sure this is safe?" I asked Gabriel.

"Yeah. We've all got active braking systems. He reassured me with a pat on the back. "There's also a stop block at the end of the line just in case. Don't worry."

"Alright I'm taking off!" Charlotte called out as Ramon gave her a three second countdown.

She took a soft leap from the ledge, flying across the line. Her cheers of excitement echoed in the distance. I couldn't even see where she had landed. All I could see was green from the trees that surrounded the caves on the other side. Natalia waited for a few minutes, before she went flying across, followed my Ramon. I was next.

My skin pricked with fear as I approached the edge. Gabriel connected my harness to the trolley, making sure everything was safely secured before I zipped across. All it took was one look down, and my panic set in. My chest rose and fell with rapid breaths as I held on to the rope, clenching my eyelids closed.

Gabriel stood on the edge next to me, placing his hands on my shoulders. "Just breathe. You'll be fine." He urged to calm me down. But it wasn't working.

"I can't do this. I can't." I cried with my eyes still closed, trembling. "I'm going back."

"It's much easier and safer to zip across than to take the ladder back down. Trust me. I've done this dozens of times."

I opened my eyes, terrified of looking down again. I couldn't do this. But I knew going backwards twenty-three stories down the ladder would've been worse.

Gabriel pulled me closer. "Let's go across together."

My eyes shot up. "At the same time? No way!"

"Trust me, we'll be fine." He hooked his lanyard on to my trolley. "Hold on to me."

I glared at him like he was a lunatic. "Are you crazy? This can't be safe!"

"Just trust me." We locked eyes. The warmth of his body against mine gave me a sense of protection. I took a deep breath, wrapping my arms around his shoulders as he held the bars of the trolley with one hand, and held me with the other.

"What if we fall?" I asked, my lips trembling.

"Then I guess we'll die together." A huge grin etched across his face, and before I could take another breath, we went flying across the stunning, tropical terrain.

Chapter 11

I felt weightless as we soared across, the warm wind brushing against my skin. My heart pumping fast.

"We're going in!" Gabriel yelled as our speed decreased.

The others cheered as we descended onto the cliff, coming to a slow halt. My fingers clenching the back of his t-shirt.

"See, that wasn't so bad." Gabriel said, He still held on to me as I caught my breath, coming down from my state of euphoria.

"That was… amazing." I said between gasping breaths. We both broke out into laughter. The others surrounded us as we unhooked our trolley from the line.

"Are you crazy!" Charlotte exclaimed with wide eyes. "You could've been killed! Both of you!" She slapped Gabriel's arm.

"You one armed it the whole way!? Dude, you're a legend!" Ramon high fived him. Charlotte didn't seem impressed. Her and Natalia surrounded me with hugs.

"Yay! You did it!" Charlotte gripped my shoulders grinning widely. "Even though Gabriel could've killed you both. I'm glad you enjoyed it." She shot a menacing look his way.

"I'm starving. Let's have lunch." Natalia suggested as she led the way through the cave.

There was an opening on the other end that would lead us back down the hill and to the mainland. Charlotte locked arms with me as we followed behind. I turned, looking back at Gabriel. Ramon was talking to him, but the words were going in one ear and out the other. Our eyes met, Gabriel winked at me. The corners of my mouth raised. I turned away, hiding my glowing smile behind my fingers.

***

We settled on the beach, enjoying beers and Bauru sandwiches that Natalia packed for everyone.

"Amari, are you going to the pride parade with us?" Natalia asked.

I paused mid-bite. I gazed around at the others, making sure I was on the same page and hadn't misheard. Everyone's eyes were on me, waiting for a reaction.

"You know, LGBTQ Pride. It's in August. In São Paulo." Ramon explained. Even though I was the last person who needed an explanation.

"I didn't bring it up to you yet because I wasn't sure if you were cool with that kind of thing. Being from the south and all." Said Charlotte.

"That sounds cool. Of course, I'm into it!" I said excitedly, but not with too much enthusiasm.

"Good. The majority of this country might hate us, but this is a bigot-free crew." Ramon said.

"What do you mean by us?" I questioned with raised brows.

"Ramon is a raging bisexual." Charlotte blurted out, emphasizing on the 'raging' part.

My jaw fell open. My queer radar was usually spot on, but I hadn't gotten those vibes from Ramon at all.

"Why do you always do that?" Ramon shoved Charlotte playfully, with a hint of umbrage in his voice from her unnecessary remark.

"What? You are!" She giggled, planting a smooch on his cheek. "I think it's hot." Ramon's cheeks flushed a soft pink. He returned the kiss but on her lips.

"Jesus, get a room you two." Gabriel scoffed, taking a swig of his beer.

"Are you going?" I asked Gabriel with nonchalance.

"Of course. I wouldn't miss it." He replied with a smile, before taking another sip of his beer.

A warm fondness fluttered inside of me, knowing that I could have a sense of comfort and security in the presence of these people. Especially him. I still had the barrier of my truth to hide, and one thing I knew from dealing with people back home was that queer folks and the ones who claimed to support us were not always trans-inclusive. But still, it was close enough for me.

We spent the evening just lounging in the sand, watching the tide come in as the sun began to set. Natalia, Ramon and Charlotte had smoked enough weed to gas up an elephant. All three of them laid stretched out on the blanket. Completely bombed.

"Hey, you wanna see something cool?" Gabriel asked in a hushed tone, inching closer towards me.

I cast a curious glance at him. "What is it?"

"Let me show you. Before it's too late." He insisted. His voice, soft and earnest.

My eyes scanned over at the others, who were nearly passed out. "What about them?" I asked with slight concern.

"They'll be alright. Let's go." He stood up, extending his hand out to me. I took it, irresistibly drawn to his assertiveness and ready to go wherever he wanted to take me.

He led me across the beach and towards a grassy hill that led to a cave. "Hold up." I hesitated, pulling back. "Why are we going in there?" I questioned with a raised brow.

"It's nothing scary, I promise." Gabriel assured me with a grin.

I took a deep breath and followed him inside. It was dark at first, but then a pale tint of orange light appeared from the other end. We approached the opening, and my pupils flared at the huge glowing sun setting over the crisp waters. The sky illuminated with a bold orange.

"Oh my God." I said as awe transformed my face. "I've never seen anything like this before." Gabriel and I stood near the edge.

"It's truly amazing. You won't get a view like this anywhere in Natal." Gabriel said, gazing out onto the horizon. He took a seat on the overhang. "We're not that far up, it's safe to sit."

I peered over the edge, looking down at the water beneath. It was a shorter distance down than the tower we climbed to zip line. I sat down next to him. Watching him admire the beautiful scene before us. He seemed to be more captivated by the sunset than I was.

"I was born here, on this island." He said.

"Really?"

"Yeah. My parents would bring me here every year for my birthday. My mom would take me up here to see the sunset and tell me to make a wish. My mother always believed that Fernando de Noronha was special. *A ilha onde os sonhos se realizer.* The island where dreams come true. She'd say.

I chuckled, nodding my head. "I don't believe in magical wishes and fairy tales."

"Maybe you should start." He said, staring at me with solemnity in his eyes.

My expression closed up, my eyes became glossy. All the times I wished and prayed for my life to be different, but nothing ever changed. Nothing ever got better. Some silly wish on a clifftop wouldn't suddenly make my life easier. I'd still wake up in the morning with male genitals between my legs and a hole in my heart.

"Last year, my grandmother was diagnosed with breast cancer." He said. "The doctors gave her six months." Gabriel's expression softened as he opened up to me. "After my parents died, she was all I had left. Disease seems to be a curse that plagues my family, and I couldn't deal with any more death and heartache.

I came up here and wished for her health to recover." The sides of his mouth raised, a smile beamed from his lips. "A month after that, we got good news from the doctors. They said that her cancer had gone into remission. It was a miracle."

His testimony of faith left me speechless. I had been so wrapped up in my own woes, that I didn't consider the blessings that God gave others. Even if it never happened to me. Gabriel's story gave me a slice of hope, that maybe if I kept an open mind God would one day bless me too. I closed my eyes and took a moment to manifest that hope.

"I did it." I opened my eyes, just as the sun disappeared below the horizon. "I made a wish."

"What did you wish for?"

"If I tell you, it won't come true." A smile tugged at my lips. The encompassing darkness had covered the sky, as we both sat side by side listening to the warm wind gently brushing around us. I peered down beneath us, observing the dark smooth, still water. "How deep do you think it is?" I wondered.

"Umm… about fifty feet maybe. It's not too far from the shore." Gabriel scrutinized me with his eyes. "Why do you ask?"

"Have you ever jumped?"

His forehead puckered. "No, never."

I relaxed my shoulders, my eyes still focused on the water. Gabriel said something else, but my mind didn't comprehend a word of it. My palms gripped the edge of the flat surface. My heart drummed as I leaned forward, leaping over the clifftop and heading feet first into the icy cold ocean water.

I could hear Gabriel yell my name in the distance as the wind flooded my eardrums on the way down. The water hit my skin like a million tiny pins penetrating me. I held my breath as I submerged myself underneath. I opened my eyes but there was nothing but darkness. I could feel tiny fish swimming around me, tickling my skin. I swam to the surface, right as Gabriel landed in the water to save me. But I didn't need saving. I was right where I wanted to be.

"Amari! Are you okay?" He swam towards me in a panic.

I floated on my back, gazing up at the indigo sky and remnants of thinning clouds. He reached for me, wrapping his arms around my torso and pulling me upwards.

"Why did you do that? Are you crazy?" He yelled.

"I'm okay. I can swim." I told him, turning to face him. He glared at me, fear overtook his face. He was even more adorable with the look of distress.

"Why did you do that? You almost gave me a heart attack!" He drew in a sharp breath, I could feel his heart beating rapidly against my chest.

"I didn't mean to scare you like that. I just… wanted to feel something. I'm sorry." I chuckled faintly, shivering and overwhelmed with emotion.

His bold brown eyes glinted with tenderness in them as he rested his hand on my face. He leaned inwards and our noses touched. His lips brushed against mine, kissing my quivering lips which went warm the second we connected. I didn't resist, I just took it all in.

Chapter 12

Our lips finally parted, as time seemed to have escaped us both. I don't even know how long we made out in the water. Neither of us said a word. My jaw clenched as I stared at him, the ocean suddenly felt colder.

"We should… probably get out of the water now." I suggested, shivering from the freezing temps and intense emotion from the kiss we just shared.

"Right…" Gabriel's face paled, I could see the uncertainty in his eyes. Unsure of what I was thinking or feeling. "Let's go this way, can you make it?"

"I'm good." I insisted. I followed him as we swam to the nearest stretch of land.

We reached the shore, a small area of jagged rocks and climbed out of the water. I hunched over, trying to catch my breath. Gabriel removed his shirt, ringing it out. I turned away, not wanting to give him the satisfaction of being marveled at. Not after such a bold move. I squeezed my soaked ponytail, raking through the damp strands with my fingers. Gabriel came towards me, reaching for my shoulder and peeling away pieces of seaweed that stuck to my drenched shirt. His hand moved down my arm, gripping my hand. My heart fluttered, I took his fingers between mine as we headed back towards the beach.

The others were packing up when we arrived, I pulled away from Gabriel, before they could see us holding hands. Charlotte walked towards us, she narrowed her eyes when she saw our soaked clothes.

"Where were you guys?" Charlotte questioned. "You went swimming?"

"Uh… yeah." I told her. "Can I have a towel please, I'm freezing." I held the sides of my arms as Charlotte grabbed towels for me and Gabriel.

We dried off as much as we could, I grabbed one of blankets and wrapped it around myself as we made our way back to the boat.

***

Back at the pier, tired and burned out everyone headed their separate ways. Charlotte and I headed towards her car, Gabriel stopped me as Charlotte continued ahead.

"I suppose we should talk about what happened back there?" Gabriel inclined, holding the towel that draped over his shoulder.

I picked at my nails, avoiding eye contact with the blanket still covering me. "I guess so."

"I'll call you tonight?"

I looked up at him. "Actually, I'll call you. My dad doesn't allow late phone calls."

"Amari, are you coming or what?" Charlotte interrupted. She hung her head out of her driver seat window.

"Coming!" I grunted, rolling my eyes. "I'll see you later." I said to Gabriel with a smile as I turned to head back to the car.

"Amari wait…" He said. I stopped, turning back around. "When we were in the water, you said that you just wanted to feel something…" He gave a soft smile, rolling his shoulders. "I hope you felt something."

Warmth covered my cheeks as intense desire blossomed within me. I bit my bottom lip, holding back a bashful grin. "Maybe." I teased, turning and heading to Charlotte's car. Maybe was a lie. I felt everything.

***

We pulled up to my father's house, Charlotte leaned over, hugging me before I got out. "I'm glad you had fun." She said.

"It was awesome." I said. "Thanks for inviting me."

We broke out hug, Charlotte's expression dulled. She cleared her throat, swooping a lock of hair behind her ear. "I know you like Gabriel."

My stomach knotted, I sat there with my hand on the door latch. This was awkward, but it was only a matter of time before she caught on.

"Okay…" I admitted with confidence, giving her space to air out whatever was on her mind, but letting her know that her opinion was insignificant.

"I want you to know that I'm not mad. It's cool." She shrugged.

"Are you sure?" I questioned in a phony tone of voice.

"Yeah, I promise. It's no biggie. Pinky swear." She smiled, holding out her pinky finger. I clamped mine around hers. Something about her sudden approval of me liking Gabriel was off-putting. Coming from someone who didn't even think I was attractive enough for him just a few days ago, it just felt forced and insincere. But it didn't matter anyway. Her approval was pointless.

"See you at the village on Monday!" I exclaimed with a grin, as I exited her car. I waved before she pulled off, and I headed inside.

I laid in bed with my elbow propped on my pillow, staring at the phone on my nightstand. I wanted to call Gabriel, but shame spiraled though me. We kissed, and a part of me felt like I had led him into a lie. But it wasn't entirely my fault. He was the one pursuing me, I was just a hormonally driven girl acting on emotion, like any other. But regardless of how I felt, I knew I couldn't allow this bond to go any farther. Not without being honest.

My stomach churned at the thought of telling Gabriel I was trans. Envisioning the look of hate and disgust on his face. Then the others finding out... it was too much to bear. Being tolerant of trans people and being personally or romantically involved with them were two completely different things.

I grabbed the phone from the hook and tossed it across the floor. Tears flooded my eyes as I slouched underneath the covers, pressing my eyes closed to rid my mind of those horrible thoughts.

It just wasn't fair. All I wanted was to be loved. Like my father used to love my mother. Like the girls in the movies I watched growing up. No matter how much Gabriel liked me, the truth would always keep me from knowing what that felt like.

Chapter 13

That week at Coloma, Charlotte and I had planned activities with the local children to teach them about nutrition and personal hygiene. I was starting to enjoy my time working in the village and understood why my father told me it was life changing for him. I felt like I was making a difference in the lives of these people, even if my impact was small.

I hadn't seen Gabriel in three days, not since our night on the island. My father told me that he wasn't feeling too well and took a few days off to rest. I tried calling him, but no one answered. I even asked Charlotte if she had heard from him, but she hadn't.

I felt like she held some resentment towards Gabriel and me for liking each other. She seemed apathetic towards his whereabouts and my feelings when I asked. It was childish, but it was her problem, not mine. We concluded our lesson for the day, clearing out the room and organizing our supplies for tomorrow's lesson. I heard the door creak open, I looked up and saw Gabriel standing there, waving for me to come over. I lightly sighed with relief. It felt good to see him again, even though I still had to break the news about us not seeing each other anymore. I walked over, opening the door and greeting him with a forced smile.

"Hey, what's been up with you?" I asked anxiously.

"I was a bit ill the past few days. But I'm feeling better now." The sides of his mouth raised, he placed his hand on my chin, but I brushed it away. His smile faded.

"I'm glad you're feeling better." I struggled to maintain my fake smile, my eyes hung to the floor. "Let's go somewhere, to talk in private."

I could feel his mood shifting. "Sure." He obliged.

We went outside, and around to the side of the building where no one else was around. I hunched over, my heart sank as I cut right to the chase.

"Gabriel, we can't see each other anymore." I admitted.

Sadness clouded his features, his eyebrows lowered. "I don't understand, I thought you liked me."

I took in a deep breath. "I do like you."

"Then why can't we see each other anymore?"

"It's complicated."

He folded his arms, smirking at me. "What could possibly be so complicated?"

"I'm not who you think I am. You wouldn't understand."

"How do you know?"

"I just do!" I snapped. My eyes began to water, I pinched the bridge of my nose. "Don't make this harder than it has to be." My voice quivered. "Just stay away. Please."

We were both silent, a weight settled on my heart. Gabriel's eyes bored into me, his jaw clenched.

"Okay." He uttered, disappointment sagged from his voice. "If that's what you want, then I'll stay away. But I just want you to know that whatever it is, it won't change how I feel about you." He reached for my limp hand, grazing my hand with his thumb. "I'm not perfect either. We've all got baggage, and life is short."

I moved my hand away. "Goodbye Gabriel." I turned and rushed back inside, wanting to get as far away from him and my heartache as I could.

***

I sat at the dinner table with my fist rested on my chin, twirling my fork around the noodles on my plate. Gabriel and I hadn't spoken since our break-up, if I could even call it that. We would see each other at the village, I'd catch him looking and pretend not to notice. Sometimes running into him was unavoidable, I'd just say hello and go on about my day. Most days I hid behind my smile, but deep down I missed him, and I never stopped thinking about the kiss we shared.

"Are you gonna eat today?" My father asked, glancing up from his plate.

"I'm not that hungry." I said, still twirling around my food.

"You've been like this for a few weeks now. Is it your meds?"

"No, my meds are fine. I'm fine."

He sat his fork down, folding his arms and proceeded to stare at me. "What's his name?" He ordered.

My posture straightened. "What are you talking about?"

"Your mood has changed. A few weeks ago, you were giddy and smiling. Up late on the phone. Now you're barely touching your food. I know it's a boy. So, what's his name?"

"It's nobody." I said unconvincingly. But he wasn't buying it. I sighed heavily, pushing my plate away. "I met someone through Charlotte. We had a thing but it's over now. No big deal."

He ran his tongue around his gums, squinting at me. "Do you want to tell me what happened?"

"I really, really don't. Can we just drop it? Please?" I begged.

"Okay. But I'm here if you wanna talk about it."

The phone rang, at what felt like perfect timing because I was getting irritated. My father got up to answer the cordless in the living room.

"Mama! It's good to hear from you!" I heard my father greeting cheerfully. I peeped my head into the living room. "Yeah, she's in the kitchen, I'll put her on." He continued.

I got up from the table and headed in the other room to get the phone. "Hey Grandma Dee!" I greeted excitedly as I took the phone from my father.

"Amari, baby! How are you?" My grandmother asked.

Hearing her gentle voice really lifted my spirits. My grandmother Darlene was one of my biggest supporters during my transition. Unlike other distant family members, grandma never spoke negatively about how I lived my life. There were things she didn't fully understand at first, but it just made her the more willing to learn and bond with me. The letters she sent me while I was in jail also kept me sane.

"I'm good grandma! Things are better."

"I can't believe you went all the way to Brazil with your daddy!" She giggled.

"I know. I can't believe it either."

"So, have you made any friends? I hope everyone has been nice to my granddaughter."

"I've made a few friends…" I looked back in the kitchen, to make sure my father wasn't listening. But just to be safe, I decided to finish our conversation in the privacy of my bedroom. "…and I met a boy." I continued as I reached my door.

"Oh! A boy! That's great honey! I bet he's handsome!"

"He is. Really cute, and so sweet. He treats me really nicely. I've never met a guy like him before."

"Sounds like things are getting serious! I'm happy for you baby girl."

"Well, we kinda broke up."

"Broke up? Why?" She questioned. I didn't say anything, and grandma automatically knew what that meant. "Oh dear, he didn't take it well, did he?"

"I haven't told him. I got scared and told him we couldn't see each other anymore."

"Well, doesn't sound like you gave him a chance honey."

"How can I? You know what's it's like for people like me. Telling him or anyone about who I am can be devastating, and dangerous."

"I understand, and I'm sorry. I wish you didn't have to hide."

"Me too. But, that's my life."

"You know, before I met your granddaddy, I had a friend. We were around your age. Times were much different then. But if I could go back and change anything, I would have taken a chance and lived my life differently."

"Why didn't you?"

"I wasn't brave. Not like you are. You're a beautiful, unapologetic young woman and any young man would be lucky to have you. Regardless of what your birth certificate says."

"Thank you Grandma."

"You only have one life to live. If you give up now, you'll regret it. Give him another chance. If he's meant for you, God will let you know."

"You really think so?"

"I know so."

"Thanks grandma."

"Alright now honey, put your daddy back on. Love you."

"Love you too. Hold on…" I went to give my father back the phone. But my grandmother's words stuck with me.

***

My father and I relaxed on the sofa, watching reruns of Martin dubbed in Portuguese with English subtitles. My father was cracking up, and even I had to admit that it was pretty comical watching one of our favorite shows in a foreign language. There was a knock on the door, my father grabbed the remote to turn the volume down, as we both shared a confused glance wondering who it could've been this time of night. He got up and headed towards the door, peeking through the peephole before opening it.

"Hello Gabriel" My father greeted. "What brings you by so late?"

"Hello Mr. Davis. My apologies, I know it's late. Is Amari awake? I was hoping we could talk."

My father glanced at his watch. "It's nine o'clock. What's so urgent?"

"It's nothing urgent, I didn't mean to disturb."

I jolted up, heading over to the door. A smile slipped when Gabriel laid eyes on me. My father turned his head to me, a line etched between brows. I knew he was putting two and two together.

"It's not that late. I'm wide awake. Can he stay for a few minutes?"

My father exhaled heavily, standing with his hand on one hip. His eyes peered into my soul. "You have an hour. Not a minute more."

"I appreciate it Mr. Davis." Gabriel said. My father gave him a nod of approval.

"Let's go to my room." I suggested, leading the way.

"That door stays open. I mean it." My father demanded.

"Yeah I know." I told him condescendingly as Gabriel and I headed down the hall to my bedroom. "What are you doing here?" I asked in a low voice, closing my door slightly so we could get a smidge of privacy.

"I know you told me to stay away, but, it hasn't been easy." He reached into the bag he was holding and pulled out a folded fabric with rainbow colors. "I was wondering if you were still going to Pride with us?"

"Yeah. But that's not until August." I said, my eyes focused on the cloth he was holding. "What's that?"

He began to unfold it. It was a long satin scarf with the colors of the pride flag flowing from one end to the other. There was a letter A stitched in the middle. He held it out to me.

"My grandmother made this for you," He said. "It's for the parade. She said you'd like it." I took it from his hands, running my fingers across the smooth fabric. "I was going to wait until I saw you at the village but, I really wanted to see you tonight."

"It's a beautiful scarf." I wrapped it around my shoulders. "I do like it. Thank you." I smiled.

That warm, fuzzy feeling came back again. I thought about the conversation I had with Grandma Dee about giving Gabriel a chance. She said that God would send me a sign. I looked into his eyes, running my fingers between the scarf and wondering if maybe this was it.

Gabriel inched closer, squeezing the empty bag underneath his arm. "I haven't stopped thinking about that night, when we kissed."

My eyes lowered, I removed the scarf from around my neck. "Me either. But you shouldn't have come here."

"I came here because I want to know who you really are."

"No, you don't." I retorted.

"What are you so afraid of?"

"Everything." My eyes began to burn, I could feel the tears forming at my eyelids. I sat at the edge of my bed, placing the scarf down next to me. Hiding my gender identity was a part of my survival. I was risking my life every single day that I existed on this earth. This wasn't just about the feelings I had for Gabriel, but also my safety. Telling him the truth could only go two ways, and the odds were never in my favor. Gabriel came over, taking a seat beside me. He placed his hand on top of mine.

"Unless you're a serial killer, there's nothing you could tell me that would make me think any less of you." His hand gripped mine.

I held my breath, fear twisted my gut as I breathed out slowly. "I was born… different."

"You mean like, with a tail or something?"

"No, nothing like that." I lightly slapped his knee. We shared a laugh. His humor and lightheartedness gave me hope that maybe he would take it well. Or at most, he wouldn't react violently. Worse case, he'd no longer want me romantically. But I was willing to sacrifice a romantic love for a platonic one.

"Maybe, it'd be easier if I just showed you?" I suggested.

"Okay, sure." He agreed.

I'll be right back. I left the room and headed towards my father's bedroom. I peeked down the hall, and just as I figured, he was still in the living room, with the TV on full blast. I tip toed towards his room, opening the door and heading for his dresser. I grabbed his wallet that sat on the top, unfolding it and reaching inside one of the back pockets.

Tucked inside was a photo of me before my transition. I was five years old. My first day of school. 'Mari's first day. '85 was written on the bottom in black marker. I hadn't seen a photo of my old self in years. A bitterness filled my mouth. I took the photo out and noticed another photo of me next to it. One I took at sixteen with Grandma Dee before my father left for the Corps. I knew he kept my childhood photos, but I didn't know he still had this one. Joy blossomed within me, the bitterness I felt went away. I closed the wallet and headed back to my room with the other photo in my hand.

Gabriel stood up when I came back in, his hands in his pockets as he drew nearer. I could feel my heart in my throat as clutched the photo between my palms. I held out my hand, with the photo facing downward. He reached for my hand, taking the photo. He glanced at me before flipping it over. I watched him, standing there. His eyes studying the picture. He was completely expressionless. My scalp prickled with panic.

"That's me…" I trembled. "When I was kid."

He looked up from the photo, his jewel-like eyes gazed over me. "Is that it?" He asked, his tone complacent.

I rubbed my forearms, hesitating with pressed lips. "Yeah. That's it."

He handed the photo back to me. "Thank God you're not a serial killer." His lips curved into a smile.

I broke into a blissful, whole hearted laughter. A tremendous weight had been lifted from my heart and my shoulders. I held the photo against my chest, I let out a breath that I didn't even realize I was holding. Gabriel wrapped his arms around me in a comforting embrace. I curled my arms around him, nuzzling my face between his neck and shoulder. Grandma was right. This was really it.

"So, how about that second date now?"

Chapter 14

We sat at the top of my bed, our backs leaned against the headboard. I rested my head on Gabriel's arm, our fingers locked together. This was the first time I had openly revealed to someone outside of my family that I was trans. I never thought in a million years that someone like him, a straight cis man would accept me so willingly. I had spent the past few weeks being coy about my feelings for him, trying to protect my heart due to my fear of the unknown. But now that it was all out in the open, I was ready to experience everything that love had to offer.

"Do the others know?" Gabriel asked.

"No. You're the only one." I said.

"Are you planning to tell them?"

"I don't know. I'm still in a bit of shock from telling you."

"You don't have to tell them, I won't say anything. I mean, it's your choice. I'm not ashamed. If you were worried about that."

"It's one of my concerns. But my choice to come out to Charlotte and the others has nothing to do with us having a relationship. I'm just selective about who I open up to in general."

"I respect that."

"Have you ever dated a trans girl before?"

" Umm, I don't think so."

"What do you mean?"

"I mean that I don't go around checking people's genital area if I'm attracted to them."

"So, you're bisexual then?"

"I didn't say that. I don't believe in labels. Sexuality is a wide spectrum. We don't always have to place ourselves in boxes."

He was right. Even being a trans woman, I found myself challenging my own ignorance towards how people choose to identify themselves. He was attracted to me, and that's all I needed to know.

"I should probably tell you that I'm not… fully transitioned." Heat flushed my cheeks.

Revealing the pre-op part of my trans life was still a challenge. Men could be attracted to me but when it came down to it, I wasn't a woman below the waist.

"Do you want to get the surgery?"

"More than anything." I flashed back to the day I sat in that hospital bed. "But it's so expensive. I'm not sure it'll ever happen. I almost had my chance, but everything fell apart when I went to jail."

"If it doesn't happen, you'll still be who you are. No matter what your birth certificate says." He held my hand tighter.

He leaned over, bringing his face closer to mine. Our lips touched, and my flesh tingled. Passion took hold of me, I was completely submerged in our kiss.

"Your hour is up." My father grumbled, standing at my half-opened door with his hand on the knob.

Gabriel and I pulled away from each other, rising up from my bed. "Must've lost track of time." I lied, heading towards the door. "I'm gonna walk him out." I told my father as Gabriel and I scooted past him, leaving my room.

"I'll see you at the Village tomorrow Mr. Davis. Thanks for inviting me in." Gabriel expressed politely.

"Have a good night Mr. Santos." My father gave him a mock salute.

I walked Gabriel out the front door, our hands clung together. He planted a kiss on my forehead. "I'll see you in the morning."

"Bye." I said breathlessly, letting go of his hand as he headed to his truck. I stood there on the porch, watching him drive away. My heart felt full and my emotions had intensified. I just wanted him to be near him again, laying comfortably within his arms. When his truck was out of sight, I headed back inside. My father stood near the hallway, staring at me with a glazed look on his face and folded arms.

"Gabriel huh?" He pondered, before giving me any signs of approval. Not that it would make a difference. "Interesting. I thought him and Charlotte were an item."

My eyes rolled to the back of my head. "Well they aren't." I stated smugly. "Good night dad." I treaded past him, trying to get to my room before he attempted a lecture.

"Wait a minute…" He called out to me. My father came closer, lowering his head. "Gabriel is a good kid. I like him. I really do. But I want you to be careful."

"Oh my God." I sneered, huffing loudly. "He knows I'm trans, dad." His expression softened, but I couldn't tell if it was a look of slight surprise or relief. "So, if you're worried about that, don't be. He accepts me."

His lips cracked a smile. "I'm glad sweetheart." His smile faded just as quickly. "But still, I'm telling you this because you're my child and I love you. I don't want to see you get hurt."

"Why can't you just let me have this? Without being negative?" Annoyance flared in me as my muscles tensed. I knew he would find some issue with me and Gabriel, which is one of the reasons I hid it from him.

"I'm not being negative."

"Yes, you are! This is the first time a boy has ever cared about me! The first time I've ever felt like this about anyone! Why can't that be enough?" I threw my hands in the air. I took a deep breath, rubbing my temple. "You weren't even around. For any of this. For anything I went through." I reminded him.

The look of devastation swept across his face. "Amari, that's not fair."

"I'm going to bed now. I have a headache." I said in a dry tone, trying to hold back tears as I left him standing there and continued to my room. My father didn't understand what it was like for me. This relationship with Gabriel was the blessing that I longed for, and I wasn't about to let my father ruin it.

Chapter 15

The next night, I couldn't wait for my date with Gabriel. He was taking me to his house to have dinner then we were going to explore the town afterwards. I stood in my bathroom mirror applying my mascara when my father knocked on the door.

"He's here." My father said.

I made sure my lashes were even before putting the tube away and opening the door. "You look nice sweetheart." He complimented.

"Thanks daddy." I replied with a short half-smile. After I yelled at him the night before, we hadn't said much to each other that whole day. I was still a little resentful about him not being immediately supportive of me dating Gabriel.

"Before you guys head out, I just want to tell you that I really am happy for you." He reached for my face, brushing his thumb across my cheek. "I'm just not used to you being so grown up."

"I know." Guilt came over me, I hugged him. "Sorry I yelled at you yesterday."

"It's alright." He assured, squeezing me gently. "Now go have fun."

We walked out into the living room where Gabriel was waiting near the sofa. His face lit up with a smile, and it seemed like the universe stopped. Everything inside it stood still, except my heart which was suddenly beating like a heavy drum.

"You look lovely." He complimented, greeting me with a hug.

"So do you." I replied, so absorbed in his brown eyes I didn't even take a second look at what he was wearing.

"Tell Miss Marcia I said hello, and don't keep Amari out too late." My father said to Gabriel.

"Bye dad!" I waved as we headed out the door and to Gabriel's truck.

***

When we arrived at Gabriel's house, a heavy aroma of savory spices filled my nostrils. "That smells amazing. What is it?" I asked.

"Feijoada and collard greens." Gabriel said, leading us to his kitchen.

My eyes widened, followed by a slight squint. "What you know about collards?" I questioned in a flippant manner.

"A lot actually. You've got a lot to learn about us Brazilians and our abundant culture. By the end of the summer, you won't want to leave." He smiled, hanging his arm around me and pulling me closer. My heart skittered. If anything kept me here, it wouldn't be the collards.

"Cheira boa avó. Food smells lovely grandma." Gabriel said as we entered the kitchen. Marcia stood at the counter, putting small balls of dough on a greased oven pan.

"Why thank you my grandson." She turned towards us, beaming with excitement when she saw me. "Olà Amari! So glad to see you again!" She welcomed me with open arms, kissing my cheek.

"Good to see you again Miss Marcia!" I greeted.

"I hope you liked my gift, it will look lovely on you at the parade."

"I did love it, thank you."

She held my forearms, grinning excitedly. "I told him you would. I'm so glad you decided to come, Gabriel really likes you. You should've seen the way he looked when he told me that you two kissed. I've never seen him so love-struck."

My eyes darted towards Gabriel, who was blushing red.

"Okay grandma, that's enough." He expressed gruffly. "Amari, why don't we go to my room while grandma finishes up in the kitchen." He suggested, latching on to my shoulder and escorting me out of the kitchen."

"Don't have too much fun." She teased. "Dinner will be ready soon." She announced as we walked away.

"Love-struck huh?" I mocked with a wide smile as we headed towards his room.

"Grandma likes to exaggerate things." He opened the door, turning on the lamp that sat next to it. A large map of the United States hung on his wall across from his bed. Red pins were placed in specific spots throughout.

"What's this for?" I asked, walking over to it to get a closer look.

"That's just a little something I started a few years ago. Places I want to visit in the states."

There were pins in New York City, Los Angeles, Orlando Florida and other small cities along the east coast. Even one in Montgomery Georgia.

"When are you planning to visit?" I asked eagerly, running my fingers along the map.

"I haven't decided yet. I've been saving money for a long time, but life seems to get in the way." He grimaced as he approached my side.

I turned to him, he raised his downcast eyes, shrugging slightly. I rested my head against his arm. "I know how it feels. You'll get there. I know you will." I wrapped my arms around his torso. "Where do you want to go first?"

"New York. Grandma told me stories of her time there when she was young. It's always been first on my bucket list."

"Maybe we could go together. I've never been."

"I'd love that." He placed his arm around me.

"We could visit all these places together. Just spend a year traveling all over." Having Gabriel in my life, gave me a sense of confidence that I hadn't had before. I felt like I could do anything or go anywhere.

"I'd love to spend a year traveling with you." He pressed his lips to my temple. "Or two… or three."

I simpered and smiled. "We're getting a little ahead of ourselves, don't you think?"

"No such thing." He insisted. "We only get to live once. Nothing is as farfetched as it seems unless you want it to be."

"I wish I had your level of optimism."

"Says the girl who jumped from a cliff."

"I knew I wasn't going to die."

"I didn't." He faced me. "I didn't know what to expect when I jumped in that water after you. But once we were in it, and I kissed you, I knew I was exactly where I was meant to be." He stroked the inside of my palm with his finger.

My eyes glinted. passion radiated between us. "So did I." I reached over and grabbed a pin from the desk that sat inches away from where I was standing. My cheeks dimpled as I grinned softly. "So, where should we go first?"

Chapter 16

After dinner, Gabriel and I headed down to the boardwalk where a small festival was taking place. The entire area was scattered with locals and tourists eating street food and enjoying the sounds of Samba. We took a stroll, passing by vendors set up along the boardwalk selling handmade jewelry, clothing and other trinkets. One of the vendors had a cart filled with beautiful, earth-tone colored beaded necklaces. I stopped, picking up one from a display hook.

"How much for this?" I asked, holding up the necklace. The old man leered at me, he didn't respond. "Excuse me, how much?" I repeated.

"não está a venda." He grunted.

"What do you mean they aren't for sale?" Gabriel retorted.

The old man reached out and snatched the necklace from my hands. "No sale!"

"What the hell!" I snapped. My face twisted with gritted teeth. I knocked over the necklace display, which caused a chain reaction of all the other jewelry displays to tumble over. Beads spilled to the ground, the old man jumped frantically from his chair. He shouted obscenities as he scrambled to pick them up. Gabriel kneeled to help him. While they were both occupied, I eyed a turquoise necklace that sat on the table. I quickly peered over my shoulder as I slid the necklace into my pocket.

"Gabriel, let's go!" I reached for his arm, pulling him away as we ran from the vendor stand.

We ran through the crowd and down to the beach, stopping to catch our breath once we were far enough out of sight. "You are so lucky no cops were around." He said through gasping breaths.

"I know right!" I pulled the necklace from my pocket. "Good thing there were none."

Gabriel's eyes sagged. A look of displeasure swept over his face. "I can't believe you stole that."

My rush of adrenaline had dissipated and transformed into shame. Gabriel reached underneath his shirt, pulling something from the waist of his pants.

"Now who am I going to give this to?" He dangled the same turquoise necklace between his fingers.

My eyes grew wide. I reached for the necklace. He grinned, playfully pulling it away from my reach. "How did you even get that without him seeing you?"

"I told you, I'm a pro." He draped the necklace over my head, gently pushing my hair away from my shoulders.

I twirled the beads around with my thumbs, gazing into his eyes. "I thought your criminal days were behind you?" I teased with a crooked smile.

"For you, I'll make an exception." He rested his hand on my chin. "That guy was an asshole. Besides, how else will we make a living when we spend a year traveling across the U.S.?"

"Now you're getting carried away." I laughed. "I'm never going back to jail. Not even for you."

"Relax, I'm only kidding."

"I know…" I sat down in the sand, kicking off my sandals and burying my feet in the warm sand. I laid back, facing up at the dark sky. Gabriel laid down next to me, propping himself up with one elbow.

"What was it like? Being in jail?" He gazed down on me.

Embarrassment coiled around me as thoughts of my imprisonment flooded to the surface. I hadn't told anyone, not even my parents about what went on while I was locked up. I felt dull and heavy, unsure if I was ready to unleash my trauma onto him.

"Or… we don't have to talk about anything at all. We can just lay here." He suggested.

"No, it's okay. I'm glad you asked. The day I was arrested, being hauled away in that cop car my first thought was if they would put me in a male prison. When I was found guilty, my lawyer begged the judge to reconsider my placement. But he just laughed in my lawyer's face." Jail was a part of my past that I wanted to leave behind, but it was time I opened up to someone and allowed myself space to heal. I cringed inwardly, remembering her wicked laugh when all we wanted was an ounce of mercy. I sat up, lifting the side of my blouse. Right below my breast was a scar.

"Oh my God…" Gabriel's forehead creased, his eyes observed me and my disfigured flesh.

"My first day in jail, my cell mate wanted to see if my breasts were real." Tears began to flood my eyelids. I pulled my shirt back down, choking back the tears of my memories. "That was just the beginning. I was beaten in the showers, sodomized with broom handles. I stabbed a guy with a fork just so the guards would throw me in solitary confinement."

I hung my head, huddled up with my arms wrapped around my legs. I forced down the bitterness that filled my mouth.

"I stayed in there for a week. It was the safest, yet scariest seven days of my life. But when it was over, I knew I had to get it together and fight back or I wouldn't make it."

Gabriel covered me with his arms. "I'm so sorry you had to go through any of that."

"I did what I had to do to survive. I used my vulnerabilities to my advantage and attached myself to the right people. I became what they wanted, what they craved from the outside. I was… nothing but a prop. A toy." I grieved, my voice dry and brittle.

"That's not who you are. You're nobody's prop, or toy." His thumb brushed the corner of my eye, wiping a single tear. "You're a person. A beautiful person who loves sappy American movies, gyros and swimming in ice cold ocean water under the moonlight."

We shared a laugh. I looked at him, smiling at me. His charm radiating hope and love onto me. I twirled the beads of the necklace that hung around my neck, reaching into my pocket where I had stuffed the other one and pulling it out.

As thrilling as it was, stealing the necklaces was both childish and reckless of us. I didn't want to end up where I was before, and I didn't want that for him either. I removed the necklace from my neck, holding both in my hands. A group of small children were playing nearly, I got up and walked over to them.

"Ola!" I greeted as I approached two of the little girls. I kneeled, holding out the two necklaces. Their eyes sparkled with joy as they took the necklaces from my hands, tossing them over their heads.

"Obrigado!" They thanked with beaming smiles, admiring the shiny pellets.

"Seja bem-vindo!" I blew the girls a kiss. "Enjoy!" I headed back towards Gabriel who stood there watching me, his mouth curved into a smile.

"You're amazing, you know that?"

"I'm alright I guess." I shrugged with a smile.

"No, I mean it." He slowly took me into his arms, resting his head on my shoulder. "I don't want this summer to end."

I held him close to me. "Me either." I said softly, taking in the subtle scent of his warm skin. Wishing this moment could last forever.

Chapter 17

My summer seemed to fly by as a month had passed. It was the end of July, and Charlotte's 22nd birthday.

"Ouch! Don't burn my ears please!" Charlotte pleaded as I stood over her holding my steaming hot curling iron.

"Girl I got this. Just hold your ear down like I told you too." I said, clamping on to a lock of her hair.

She reached over, grabbing a photo from my dresser. It was a picture of Gabriel and I at the carnival in Sao Luis. "You two are adorable." She complimented, placing the photo back down. "I hope you don't mind me asking, but I gotta know…"

My brows knitted together. "Know what?"

"You know…" Her voice trailed off. She grinned at me through the mirror. "What's the sex like?"

My curling iron grazed her ear. her shoulders tightened as she shrieked from the sting. "My bad!" I consoled through gritted teeth. I tensed up, unprepared for this intimate discussion. "That's none of your business." I responded.

"Aww come on! Tell me! I tell you about Ramon. Spill the beans!" She begged.

I chuckled awkwardly. "There's nothing to tell."

"Oh please!"

"I'm being serious!" I assured her, and it was the truth. In the month that Gabriel and I had been together, nothing ever went beyond kissing. It was a mutual understanding between the both of us that we wouldn't rush into anything serious. Which would've been more believable to Charlotte had she known about me being trans.

"I don't believe you one bit. That must mean he's bad in bed. Guess I dodged a bullet then." She shrugged. He's coming to my party right?" She asked. "I called him yesterday, but Marcia said he wasn't home."

"Yeah, he's coming, as far as I know." I hadn't spoken to Gabriel since yesterday afternoon and Charlotte's party was in an hour. He told me that he had some business to take care of and would be gone for the day. I called him this morning, but no one answered.

"Can we take a break? I gotta pee." Charlotte got up from her chair and headed to my bathroom.

I sat my curlers down and went over to grab my cordless phone. I decided to call Gabriel again. It just rang and rang. No answer. My heart felt uneasy. He should've at least called once by now. I hung up and redialed his number but hung up again before the third ring. I took a deep breath, not trying to assume the worst. I'd at least wait until the party before I worried too much.

I finished Charlotte's hair and we got dressed and prepared to head to her house before everyone started arriving. We headed to her car, she stopped before reaching the driver's side.

"Dammit." Charlotte dug through her purse, huffing loudly. "I left my keys in your room. I'll be right back." She said, trotting back inside my house in her platform heels.

I got inside and pulled open the sun visor to reapply my lip gloss in the mirror while I waited. She finally came back, getting in the car without saying a word. While we were getting ready she was her usual chipper self, eager to party. But her mood seemed to have gone flat.

"You alright?" I inclined.

"Yep." She replied in a chary tone, starting the car and driving off swiftly.

***

The party was mostly PCV's and other locals that were associates of Charlotte. I hung out in the backyard with Natalia while Charlotte entertained other party guests in her living room playing beer pong. I glanced at my watch, inhaling heavily as my leg shook repeatedly. Another hour had gone by and still no sign of Gabriel. I was becoming more agitated than worried, wondering what the hell was up with him. The alcohol was calming my nerves, but I was down to my last drop and needed the distraction.

"I'm gonna go get another drink. Be right back." I told Natalia as I headed back inside and towards the kitchen. I squeezed passed their drunken game of beer pong, and that's when I saw him, standing near the stairs with a beer in his hand. I sighed with relief, making my way over him.

"Hey!" I greeted cheerfully, locking my arm around him in a hug. But my joy in seeing him was short lived, and I was more annoyed that he seemed to be dodging me.

"Hey." He said in a low voice, giving me a limp hug back.

"When did you get here?" I asked.

"Like thirty minutes ago." He said nonchalantly, dangling the beer bottle from his hand.

I frowned, pulling away. "You've been here for thirty minutes and you didn't bother to come and find me?"

"Find you for what? I knew you were here." He took a swig of his beer, his attention turned away from me.

My face scrunched up as I stared at him. His off-handed tone was making me uncomfortable and something about him didn't feel right. His eyes were red and weary, his face looked a bit worn out and he reeked of alcohol.

"What's going on with you?" I questioned angrily.

"Nothing." He took another sip of his beer.

My jaw clenched as I folded my arms. This indifferent attitude of his was pissing me off and starting to hurt my feelings. "Something is going on. I haven't heard from you all day. I was worried and now you show up here without even telling me… and you're drunk? You never drink this much." My voice began to raise.

"I told you that I would be busy. Why are you overreacting?"

"Overreacting?" I scoffed. "Well sorry if me caring means I'm overreacting!"

"Well maybe you should care a little less then." He said in a smug tone.

Charlotte made her way over to us. "Oh look, it's the love birds!" She pranced over towards us. "What are you guys talking about?" She pried, standing with one hand on her hip.

"None of your business." Gabriel said to her.

"Of course, it isn't. Nothing is ever my business when it comes to you two." She faced me, her expression went blank. "Isn't that right… Damarion?" A devious grin formed at the edge of her lips.

My eyes lit up. My skin, cold with dread.

"That's your name isn't it?" Charlotte continued. "I saw the photo in your room. I found your passport and put two and two together. You were such a cute little boy." She said with pouted lips.

"Charlotte shut up." Gabriel warned.

"That's what she is right? Oh, I mean HE!"

"Charlotte that's enough! Get out of here!" He snapped. The room got quiet, heads turned as it seemed all eyes were on us.

"Did you know?" She scowled at him. "No, don't answer that. Of course, you did. That's why you'd never sleep with me. You're a fag!" She scolded, shoving him.

He slammed his bottle on the floor, storming off. Charlotte let out a merciless chuckle while I just stood there, speechless in a catatonic state. I felt heavy, I needed to get away from her. Out of that house, away from everyone. I ran, shoving past people as I headed for the front door. Outside, I caught Gabriel as he got inside of his truck, slamming the door closed in a rage.

"Gabriel, wait…" I ran to the truck before he could leave, grabbing on to the latch on the passenger door.

"Just stay away from me!" His hands clenched the wheel.

"Why are you being like this?" I cried.

"I should've never kissed you. I should've never let us get this far…"

My eyes went wide, glistening with tears. "What… what are you saying…" I stammered with quivering lips.

"Goodbye Amari." He started the engine, pulling away as I clung to the door latch.

"Gabriel!" I called for him, but he was gone.

Natalia came outside, rushing over to me. "Amari, are you okay?" She asked. I turned to her, nodding. My hands clutching my forearms. She approached me, placing her hand on my shoulder. "Come on, I'll take you home."

My heart plummeted to the pit of my stomach as I burst into tears. Humiliated, and heartbroken.

***

Natalia dropped me off at home, and I could see the light on in the living room as I approached the door. I went inside, my father was asleep on the couch. A wave of emotion hit me, feeling like a knife to the chest. The sound of the door closing behind me woke my father from his sleep.

He sat up, rubbing his eyes as he glanced at his watch. "The party is over already?"

I walked slowly towards him, my lips pressed together as I tried to hold it all in. My eyes began to tear up again. "Daddy…"

"Amari, what's wrong?" He stood up as I drew nearer.

"Charlotte, she…" My breath caught as I stumbled over my words.

"She what?" He sprung up from the couch. "What happened at the party?"

"She outed me…" I uttered. His eyes grew wide, his jaw clenched. "…and Gabriel, he broke up with me."

He squeezed his eyes shut, sighing heavily as I began to cry in his arms. "I can't believe she would do that to you."

"She humiliated me in front of everyone. Then Gabriel got angry and just left me there. He hates me." I sobbed.

"Hold on now, what do you mean he hates you? I don't understand. You two were just together."

I broke away from him, taking a seat on the couch. "He showed up at the party, really drunk and in a bad mood. I hadn't heard from him since yesterday morning, so I asked him what was wrong. He got mad me for asking then everything just…" I leaned over, burying my face in my hands. My father sat down next to me. "Before he left, he said that I was a mistake. That he wished we never kissed."

"I know Gabriel, he couldn't have meant that."

"Then why would he say those things to me?" I looked up at him, tears spilled from my eyelids. "I though he loved me."

"I can't answer that baby girl." He wrapped his arm around me. "But I do know one thing, there isn't an ounce of hate in that boy. Whatever he's going through, I don't think it has anything to do with you."

"I know you're just trying to make me feel better, but it still hurts."

"I know, and I hate to see you like this." He held me tighter. "Just give him some space. I'm sure he'll come around."

"What about the village? What about Charlotte?"

"Don't worry about any of that right now. Everything will be fine." He assured me. "You don't have to go back to Coloma if you don't want to."

I wiped my tears with the back of my hand. "I'm so glad I have you, still."

"You'll always have me. People and relationships change all the time. You know that, and I'm not gonna sugarcoat things for you." He lifted my chin, looking down at my glum face. "But your mother and I will always be here for you. That will never change."

A smile made its way onto my lips. Even through the gut-wrenching heartbreak that I was feeling over Gabriel and Charlotte, moments like this reminded me of how thankful I was to have my father's love and wisdom to keep me going.

Chapter 18

I couldn't sleep at all that night. What happened at the party kept replaying in my head like a bad movie, as I laid in bed the next morning, clutching my pillow with swollen red eyes. Each minute passed that I waited for his call, the wound on my heart grew bigger. This was real, it was over between us. There was no way I could go back to Coloma after this. Everyone knew my secret, and all the fears I had of being degraded and tormented were flooding back to the surface. I no longer felt safe, I just wanted to go back to Georgia and pretend that none of this ever happened, erasing the heartache from my memory forever.

The phone rang, my eyes darted over to the blinking light on the reciever. Gabriel? I sat up, reaching to answer. Hoping to God it was him. "Hello?"

"Amari, Good morning dear. Sorry to call so early. It's Marcia." She answered in a small panicky voice.

"Miss Marcia?" I hesitated, feeling uneasy. "Hi, what's going on?"

"I was wondering if you'd heard from Gabriel? He didn't come home last night, and I'm worried."

I tossed my covers aside, jumping out of bed. "What do you mean he didn't come home?"

"He left for Charlotte's party last night, and that was the last I saw of him. He had been drinking before he left, and I urged him not to drive but he didn't listen." She sniffled. "Please, tell me you've heard from him?"

"He was at the party last night, but we argued and he left. I assumed he went home."

"Oh no, what if he's hurt!"

"Don't worry Miss Marcia, I'll get my dad and we'll find him. I promise." I ran my palm across my face, trembling as I thought of where on earth he could possibly be or if he was even okay. Then it hit me. There was only one place that Gabriel would go at a time like this. "Stay by the phone, my dad and I are gonna try and figure this out. I think I know where he might be."

"Dear God, I hope he's safe." She began to mumble a prayer.

"Me too. I'll call you back okay?"

"Okay sweethart, thank you."

"Bye." I put the phone back and hurried out of my room to fill my father in on what was going on. I went into the kitchen where he was having breakfast.

"Morning baby girl, how are you feeling?" He asked, sipping from his coffee mug.

"Dad, Gabriel didn't go home last night. His grandmother called. She's worried, I'm worried. What if something happened to him? We have to find him!" My chest rose and fell with rapid breaths, panic began to set in.

My father got up from the table, making his way over to me. "Calm down, Amari. We'll find him. It'll be okay." He placed his hands on my shoulders, in an attempt to sooth me but my anxiety was through the roof. "Do you know where he might be?"

"Fernando de Noronha. At least I think so."

A line etched between his brows. "Are you sure?"

"His mom used to take him there when he was little. The sunset cliff. It's his happy place." I inhaled deeply to catch my breath as I tried to explain. "I just have a feeling…"

"No, not at all. This is useful information. We can start there. I'll call his grandmother back and let her know where we're going. Finish getting dressed and meet me outside when you're done."

I nodded as he planted a kiss on my forehead before leaving the kitchen to go call Marcia back. I headed back to my room to grab my shoes, hoping to God that I was right about Gabriel.

***

We drove down to the pier, and as we got close I immediately spotted Gabriel's truck parked near the dock.

"There's his truck!" I yelled with a pointed finger. My father stopped the car, I swiftly unbuckled my seatbelt, opening the door and rushing over to see if Gabriel was inside. As I approached the truck, my jaw went slack at the sight of his damaged vehicle. The front bumper was completely totaled. My father got out of the car, rushing over to me.

"Is he in there?" His eyes widened when he saw the damage. "Jesus Christ!"

I surveyed the area and noticed that Ramon's boat was missing. "Dad, Ramon's boat is gone! That means Gabriel is on the island!"

"Stay here, I'll go rent us a powerboat and call Marcia to give her an update."

I stood there holding my forearms, growing more anxious by the second while I waited. Not knowing what was going on with Gabriel was killing me. I pressed my hands against the window, peeking inside the truck. There were empty beer bottles on the floor and in the passenger seat. My heart wrenched at the sight of it. This wasn't the Gabriel I knew.

My father came back, holding a set of keys. "Alright, let's head out, and hope for the best."

We headed to the opposite end of the dock and boarded a small express cruiser. I never thought my second trip to back to such a beautiful place, would be under the worst circumstances. At this point I wasn't worried about our relationship anymore. My only concern as we sailed out to Fernando de Noronha was Gabriel's wellbeing, and getting him home safely.

***

We arrived at the island, I wasted no time exiting the boat in a hurry.

"Hold on now, not so fast." My father called out to me as he shut off the engine. "Don't go running off. We still need to look for him, together."

"I know where he is. Just follow me." I ran at a steady pace across the sand, giving my father time to keep up as he exited the boat.

I remembered exactly where the cave was that led to the cliff. The memory of our kiss, and zip lining from the lighthouse flashed in my mind as I walked through the island. It was as if I had never left. When we reached the cave, a sudden wave of fear washed over me. What if he wasn't up there? What if he jumped to his death and we were too late?

"So, this is it?" My father asked, observing the cave with a raised brow. "Want me to come with you?"

"No, let me talk to him. Alone."

My father nodded. "I'll wait here. Yell if you need me."

I went in, my muscles tensed as I reached the opening on the other side. There he was. I let out a sigh of relief as I saw him sitting at the edge. Thank God. I eased out slowly, keeping my distance so I wouldn't startle him.

"Can I sit? Or will you scream at me?" I said in a low voice.

He turned around, his brows drew together at the sight of me standing behind him. "Amari, what are you doing here?"

"Your grandmother said you didn't come home last night. She's worried sick. So am I" I inched closer, taking a seat next to him on the edge. There was dried blood on his hands. "Oh my God..." I got a look at his face, there was small gash on the left side of his forehead. "You're hurt!?" I grazed his wound with my finger. "I saw your truck. Why didn't you go to a hospital?"

"It's just a small cut. I'll be fine." He took hold of my hand, pulling it away from his face. He locked his fingers between mine, tears shone in his heavy eyes. "I didn't mean any of those things I said last night." His grip on my hand tightened. "I was just trying to protect you."

I squinted. "Protect me from what?"

"From me."

"Why would you need to do that?"

He stared vacantly out into the ocean. His lips trembled as he hesitated to speak again. "I have HIV."

My jaw dropped. Pain gripped my chest as sorrow shredded my insides. I watched him, sitting there with hopelessness spilling from his eyes.

"I went to see my doctor two days ago, and he told me that my white cell count had dropped below 500." His face fell, the emptiness he felt manifested onto him. "It won't be long before my status changes to full blown AIDS."

The pain in my chest grew tighter. "Why didn't you say anything?"

"I didn't want my illness to become your burden. I wanted your memory of us to be only good things. I didn't want you to hurt or remember me this way."

"Stop talking about yourself like that." I pleaded with glistening eyes. "Like you're dying! You're not!"

"I am, and that's okay. Not today, or tomorrow. But this virus will take me sooner than later. Just like my parents."

"How long… Do you think you have left?"

"I don't know. Could be six months. Could be six years, if I'm lucky."

My shoulders went limp as all the hope I had for him, for us, suddenly disintegrated. "It's not fair..."

"Life never is." He gripped my hand. "But I'll keep living. For now. That's all I can do." He wrapped his arm around me,

"I'll be right here with you. I promise." I buried my face into his shoulder. "I love you, Gabriel."

His fingers caressed the side of my face. "I love you too."

Chapter 19

We took Gabriel to the hospital to get his wound stitched up before taking him home. The ride back home with my father was a melancholic one. I couldn't stop thinking about Gabriel and his impending fate. My father could hear my faint cries from the backseat that I tried to hide.

"I'm sorry baby girl." He uttered from the front seat, his eyes peeking at me through the rearview mirror.

I wiped my wet face with my arm. Swallowing my quiet sobs. "Did you know?"

His eyes remained forward, he couldn't even look at me. "I did." He admitted. That sinking feeling in my chest had intensified. It seemed like everyone knew about this except me. "I've known about his status since I met him in the health program in Coloma two years ago. I didn't tell you because it wasn't my place. I worried when you two were getting close, but I trusted him to tell you when he was ready."

As upset as I was, I understood why my father kept it from me. But I was beginning to feel like maybe things would've been better, had they been left unsaid.

"You remember the talks we had, right? About HIV and AIDS?" He asked. I nodded, yes. "There are stigmas about the virus, and the people who have it. But times are changing, and people are learning to live with it. Staying healthy for years and years. Gabriel can too."

His positive affirmation had calmed me a little, but it wasn't enough to take the pain away. Gabriel knew that he was living on borrowed time. That was his reality. No matter how optimistic my father tried to be.

"I need to ask you something, and I want you to be honest with me." He said firmly.

"What?" I mumbled in a raspy tone.

"I know you don't like me asking these kinds of personal questions, but have you two-"

"No dad! Jesus Christ!" I retorted, pinching the bridge of my nose.

"Okay, okay. I didn't mean to upset you, and I'm not judging. I just want to make sure you're protecting yourself. Always."

"I don't want to talk about this anymore." I slouched down in my seat, facing the window as we rode home in silence. It hurt too much to know that Gabriel was suffering. Life was easier when it was just me doing the suffering.

When we got home, my fatigue had set in. I hadn't slept in over twenty-four hours, my arms felt disconnected and heavy. My legs felt like they were glued to the floor. I went to my room and threw myself onto my bed. I closed my heavy eyes, succumbing to my exhaustion.

***

I awoke to the sounds of a tapping against my window. I turned over, rubbing my eyes as I turned on my lamp. I peered at the clock, it was ten past midnight.

"Amari, it's me." A voice whispered from outside my window.

I recognized the voice. I got out of bed and walked over, pulling up my blinds. My eyes widened at the sight of him standing there.

"What are you doing here?" I asked, pulling up the window screen.

"I know it's really late, but I wanted to see you." Gabriel said.

"Are you trying to get me in trouble?" I said in a loud whisper. "What's going on? Are you okay?"

"I'm fine. I just couldn't sleep."

"Wait here." I walked over to my door, opening it slightly to peek through. All the lights were off, and the door to my father's room down the hall was closed. There was no light coming from beneath the door, which meant he was out for the night. I pulled my head back in, closing my door gently and locking it. I went back to the window. I grabbed his arm, helping him in as he climbed through. I closed the window, pulling my blinds back down and closing the curtains.

"I'm sorry for coming by like this. I missed you."

"Don't apologize. I'm glad you're here. Come and lay with me." I took has hand, guiding him over to the bed. We laid down next to each other, I rested my head on his chest. I could feel his warm body heat through his t-shirt as I snuggled under him.

"I've been in a bad place these last few days. I didn't mean to drag you into my disaster of a life." He said, speaking softly.

"You didn't drag me into anything. I chose this, and your life isn't any more of a disaster than mine." I looked up at him. "Can I ask you something?"

"Of course, what is it?"

"How did you get it? The virus."

He winced slightly, as memories of shame surfaced. "I was sixteen, and reckless. My girlfriend at the time was a drug addict. We never used protection and I didn't know she had the virus. After losing my parents to AIDS, I should've known better. I should've protected myself. But deep down, I don't think I really cared."

"What happened to her?"

"I don't know. She ended up running off with her dealer after I confronted her. I never saw her again. She's probably dead now."

"Did you love her?"

He shrugged. "At one point I'm sure I did. But not like I love you, now." He pressed his forehead against mine. "I should've told you about this sooner. You were brave enough to open up to me, I should've been brave enough to do the same. You deserved better."

"You did it when you were ready. I'll never hold that against you."

"You saved me by coming to Fernando. I'm not sure I'd even be here with you right now, had you not come to look for me. Having this disease is a never-ending emotional battle of not knowing when the end will be. I felt like giving up when I was on that cliff today. My grandmother watched my mom die, and I didn't want her to relive that again. But then I saw you, and I remembered that my life is beautiful." He caressed the side of my face, tracing his thumb along my eyebrow. "It's beautiful because you're in it."

His finger touched my neck, and the hair as it was moved away nearly gave me chills. I never thought I'd ever fall so deeply for someone, the way I fell for Gabriel. All this time, I wanted to know what it felt like to be the center of someone else's universe. But here I was, looking into the eyes of a beautiful boy who was the center of mine.

"I love you." He whispered.

"I love you too."

He kissed my temple tenderly, resting his cheek on my head. "I should be getting home now, before your dad wakes up."

"Or you could stay, if you want." I timidly suggested. I gripped his hand tighter, making sure we were both on the same page. "He won't wake up. We have time. Don't worry."

"Are you sure?"

"When summer ends, I don't know when or if we'll ever see each other again. I want our final days together to be special. When I said I wanted to experience everything that love had to offer, I meant it."

His eyes dug into mine. He was hesitant, but I could tell that he wanted this as much as I did. "But I'm not even prepared for that. It's been a long time."

"I got condoms from Coloma during one of the sex-ed classes. We'll be fine. It's okay, I want this."

"Only if you're one hundred percent sure. I mean it."

I wrapped my hand around the nape of his neck. "I am sure. I mean it." I removed my shirt, my lips brushed his, delicately at first. Just long enough for our bodies to become one as we shared one breath. One sensation. One timeless and passionate moment.

Chapter 20

Seven. That's how many tiny little moles I counted, embedded in his golden skin as he lay next to me. I watched him sleep, as the sun rose through my curtains. Gabriel should've been gone by now, but I couldn't let him go. I wanted to keep him close to me forever. Even if that meant never leaving my room. I was fine with that.

"Amari, are you awake?" My father called from behind my door, knocking twice.

Gabriel awoke from his sleep, I placed my hand over his mouth, sitting up swiftly. "Yes dad." I answered anxiously.

"Oh, well I just wanted to know if you were joining me for breakfast?" He jiggled the knob. "Why is your door locked?"

"Dad, I'll be out soon!" My heart thudded. I turned to Gabriel biting my bottom lip, his eyes wide.

"Alright." I could hear the floorboards creaking as he walked away.

I let out a sigh of relief, removing my hand from Gabriel's mouth. He quickly got out of bed, scrambling to get dressed. I tossed on my night shirt and a pair of shorts from the floor as Gabriel quietly opened my window. I went over, planting a kiss on his lips as he climbed out.

"See you later?" He smiled.

"Yes. Now go, before he sees you!" I said in a loud whisper, giving him another kiss as he left.

I closed the window behind him and made my way out to the kitchen. My father was sitting at the table reading the morning paper.

"Morning daddy." I greeted as I approached the table. As I pulled out my chair, I noticed that there were three plates out.

"Good morning sweetie." He pulled the paper away from his face, glancing at me, then at the third plate that sat next to mine. "Oh, I was under the impression that Gabriel would be joining us. My mistake." He said in a smug tone, his eyes peered back to the paper.

My heart sank into my stomach. I stood there, holding my forearms with hunched shoulders. The awkward silence lingered for a few seconds as I tried to muster up an excuse. There was nothing I could say to get myself out of this one.

"I took out the garbage when I woke up. I saw his truck outside." He cleared his throat, taking a bite of his eggs as he looked at me, waiting for an explanation.

"He came by while I was sleeping. He just wanted to talk. So, we just... talked." I broke eye contact.

"Okay." He continued eating with a vacant expression.

"Am I in trouble?" I asked unassumingly.

He sat his fork down, closing the paper and placing it down on the table. "Sit down and eat before your food gets cold."

I slid out my chair, sitting down cautiously as I mentally prepared myself for yet another a lecture.

My father faced me with stern eyes, asserting his authority. "I'm not happy that you snuck a boy in my house in the middle of the night, Gabriel or not." His expression softened. "But no, you're not in trouble."

"It won't happen again, I promise." I assured him, too ashamed to look him in the eyes. I didn't regret spending the night with Gabriel, but it did hurt knowing I disappointed my father.

"Listen, I know you're not a kid anymore. But I need you to meet me halfway with this parenting stuff."

"Alright."

He placed his hand on my shoulder. "I'm glad that you two found each other. You've both been through so much, you deserve to be happy." His lips formed into a heartwarming smile.

"Thank you dad." I placed my hand over his.

There was a knock on the front door. "Did your boyfriend forget something?" My father smirked.

I cut my eyes at him, as I got up and headed to the door. I opened it, there was Charlotte. Twirling the ends of her hair, standing in front of me with downcast eyes.

"Who is it?" My father asked from the kitchen.

I crossed my arms, looking at her through narrow eyes. "It's nobody." Seeing her face roiled my stomach.

"Hey." She uttered, swooping a lock of hair behind her ear.

"What do want?" I scowled, pain seeping from my voice.

I could hear my father's footsteps approaching behind me. "Charlotte, is there something you need?" He stood firmly behind me.

"Hi Mr. Davis. I know it's early, but-"

I turned to my father. "Dad let me handle this" I advised. He clenched his jaw, giving me a slight nod before walking away. I opened the screen door, stepping outside. I faced Charlotte, standing only inches away with crossed arms. "What do you want?"

"I wanted to apologize, about what happened at my party. How I acted, that's not who I am. You know me."

"That's your excuse for dead naming and humiliating me?"

"Finding that photo was a lot for me to take in. I didn't know what to think, or how to act. I let my jealously about Gabriel cloud my judgement. But I didn't mean any of it." She pleaded with glinted eyes.

"Yes, you did. People like you always mean it."

"People like me?" She gasped. "What's that supposed to mean?"

"People like you who think that you're special or tolerant just because you have gay friends or go to a few pride parades. But you're not. You're just as bigoted as everyone else."

"That's not fair. I'm trying."

I rolled my eyes. "This isn't about you, Charlotte. An apology to ease your own guilt won't change the fact that you put me and Gabriel's life in jeopardy when you outed us. Your transphobia could've gotten me killed. I'm thankful that things didn't go as bad as they could've. But even still, I'm afraid to go back to Coloma. I have to spend the rest of my summer constantly looking over my shoulder, because of you."

"I'm so sorry, Amari."

"I know you are. But I'm not interested in your apology, or your friendship right now. You should go."

With crocodile tears and pressed lips, she dragged her feet back to her car. Charlotte knew that there was nothing more she could say to mend what she had broken. I headed back inside, leaning against the closed door with slumped shoulders. sighing heavily and I went back into the kitchen. My father had finished his breakfast, standing over the kitchen sink as he washed the dishes. He paused, turning around as I sat back in my chair.

"How did everything go?" He asked.

"She apologized." I stabbed my cold eggs with my fork.

He turned the faucet off. "Then what?"

"I'm not ready to forgive her, if I ever do."

He lowered his head. "I'm sorry things had to be this way between you two. But I understand your decision."

"You're not going to give me a lecture on forgiveness?" I teased.

"No. I think you did the right thing. She'll have to live with her words and actions, and it's not your job to ease her remorse." He turned the faucet back on and continued with the dishes.

"Do I have to go back to Coloma?" I asked.

"You don't have to. But I'd prefer it if you found something to fill your time." He turned again, giving me his serious daddy glare. "Something productive."

"Yeah, yeah. I will." I gave a lopsided grin, taking feeble bites from my plate.

***

After breakfast I went back to my room to call Gabriel.

"Ola" He answered.

"Ola." My face lit up with a smile as I crawled back into bed. "I miss you already."

"I miss you too. I hope I didn't get you in trouble."

"Well, he saw your truck outside."

"Oh, shit."

"I'm not in trouble though. But no more after-hours pop ups at my window. Okay?"

"You've got my word."

"So, about last night…" I fiddled with a loose thread that stuck out from my pillowcase. "I'm glad you came over. I had a good time." I smiled.

"So did I. But, I need you to promise me something."

My smile grew faint. "Of course, what is it?"

"Promise me that you'll get yourself tested."

"Why? We were safe."

"I know. But still. I'd feel better if you did. So, promise me you will."

"Alright. I promise." This talk of getting tested was depressing me. I didn't need another reminder that the guy I loved was sick. "Charlotte came by. She tried to apologize." I told him, casually skipping the subject.

"What did you say to her?"

"I called her a bigot and told her to leave. I'm not ready to deal with her yet. Which sucks because I'll miss being at the village. But I just don't feel comfortable going back."

"Coloma won't be the same without you, but I understand. What will you do then?"

"I don't know. But my dad told me that I need to keep myself busy."

"I have a few ideas…" He suggested facetiously.

"Not like that." I giggled. "I have no idea what I'm going to do for the next four weeks."

"My Grandmother could use some help with her gardening. Her Brazilian Plume Flowers are blooming, she sells them to local flower shops. It's not much, but it'll give you something to do. She likes you and I'm sure she wouldn't mind."

I shrugged. "Yeah, I guess I could do that." I dreaded the idea of doing more physical labor in the heat. But I figured doing anything that involved spending time with Miss Marcia would be worth it.

Chapter 21

That following day, my father dropped me off at Gabriel's house before heading to work. Marcia was thrilled to have me help her garden, and I was looking forward to her lighthearted and sassy grandma shenanigans to keep me content and my mind off Charlotte. When I arrived, she opened the door as I approached.

"Good morning Amari, you look lovely in your yellow sundress today! That color really suits you!" She complimented.

I smiled. "Thank you Miss Marcia!"

"Come in, I'm just getting started." She stood aside, allowing me space to come in. "You go ahead to the backyard, I'll grab us some drinks."

"Alright." I headed out towards the back while she went inside the kitchen.

The Santos' backyard was small but cozy. Perfect for sowing and maintaining plants. To my left, were rows of bushes covered in pink flowers. The petals stuck out like little tiny fingers nestled between deep green lance-shaped leaves. Some of the flowers had already been plucked and sat in a basket in the grass. I walked over to the basket, kneeling down to grab one. I held it up to my nostrils. The fragrance was only slightly sweet, but still effective because I couldn't put it down.

"Magnificent aren't they?" Asked Miss Marcia as she came outside carrying a tray holding two glasses of sugarcane juice. "Did you know these flowers can be boiled and used to treat anemia?" She handed me a glass. "They turn a crimson red, growing up we would call it the blood of Jesus."

"Oh wow, that's so cool." I took a sip of my drink.

"I told Gabriel I'd fill your time adequately." She sat down next to me, sitting the tray on the opposite side in the grass. "I'm sorry that you won't be returning to Coloma. I'd ask why, but I'm sure it's none of my business."

I broke eye contact, peering down at my glass. Gabriel hadn't gone into detail about what happened at the party, and I'm glad he hadn't. It was embarrassing enough the first time.

"Well thanks for letting me come over and help. I appreciate it."

"It's no problem honey." She smiled. "I want to thank you again for finding my grandson and bringing him home safely. You have no idea how much I appreciate you and your father being in Gabriel's life."

"You don't have to thank me, really. I love Gabriel. You're supposed to be there for people you love."

"Gabriel told me that Charlotte had a bit of an outburst at her party. She called him the F word. All because he doesn't want to be with her. What a cadela she is! I always told him that girl was trouble. I just don't understand why the gay slur was necessary." She shook her head, gently plucking a flower from the bush and placing it in the basket.

"She called him that, because of me."

She faced me with furrowed brows. "Why would she do that?"

"Because... she found out that I wasn't born a girl."

She paused, holding one of the flowers in her hands. I could see a small grin forming at the corners of her mouth. "You know, I knew there was something different about you that night we first met. When Gabriel came back after taking you home, I said to him, that girl is special. Keep her close. I could feel it, and I was right." She playfully nudged my arm. "That's why I made that scarf for you."

"So, you knew I was trans this whole time."

"No. But I've spent enough time around women to know when one is right for my grandson. Also, between me and you, I've had way more girlfriends than him. I know my stuff." She bragged with a smirk.

"Oh, is that right?" I laughed.

"Oh, yes. I had my first girlfriend when I was twelve years old. Her name was Carla. I was devastated when her family moved to Bolivia. Not just because I liked her, but because I had never met anyone else like me before. Not until I went to the U.S. That was life changing for me."

"That photo in your living room, of you and that red-haired girl. Was she your girlfriend?"

"Rose? Yes. We were together for nine months during my year in the states. The queer community in New York City was unlike anything I had ever experienced. It felt like my true home."

"Why didn't you stay? Or go back?"

"Life didn't allow me that luxury. I thought about going back, but I ended up meeting Gabriel's grandfather one night on a drunken bender. Nine months later, I was a mom. I don't even remember his name. I think it was Raul?" She chuckled faintly.

"I'm sorry."

"Don't be. My life turned out just as it should have. If I had gone back to the states, I wouldn't have had my daughter, she wouldn't have given me Gabriel, and you wouldn't be sitting here enjoying sugarcane with me right now. If anything, my time in New York gave me the courage to live my truth."

"So, you don't have any regrets?" I asked, twirling the straw in my cup. "Not even about leaving your girlfriend in New York?"

"Life is too short for regrets. I miss the memories, but everything happens for a reason. Even the things that don't feel so good."

I thought about my life and if all the horrible things that happened to me were a part of some divine plan for my life. I guess if I had never gone to jail, I wouldn't have ended up here. Maybe she was right.

"I've thought about staying here in Brazil. But my father won't allow it, and I'd miss my mother too much. But, I love it here and I don't want to leave Gabriel." My eyes began to burn as tears stung from behind my eyelids. "I don't want to say goodbye."

"Then don't say goodbye. *Até a próxima vez*. See you next time."

"That does sound better." I patted the corners of my eyes with my thumb.

"See, it's working already." She reached for my hand. Her positivity was heartwarming and gave me hope that there could've been a future for Gabriel and me after all.

Chapter 22

The humid air passed through my fingers as I sat with my arm out the window in the passenger side seat of Gabriel's truck. The smell of the passing morning rainfall tinged my nostrils. The sadness of my final days in Brazil were settling on my heart and it was a bittersweet feeling. The small things that I took for granted when I arrived three months ago, were now gems in my heart that I wanted to last forever. The Pride celebration in São Paulo was the perfect end to an unforgettable summer.

"We're here." Gabriel pulled into a lot full of people with their cars parked inches away from one another. He parked in an empty space near the edge, getting out and coming around to my side to open my door.

"I can open my own door, you know." I teased, getting out of the truck.

"I know, but I enjoy the view." He smiled, clutching the ends of the rainbow scarf that hung from my neck. "My favorite view of all." He stroked the side of my face, leaning in for a kiss.

A smile cracked through my lips mid-kiss. "We should hurry, I don't want to miss the parade."

"We won't miss a thing, don't worry." He kissed me again.

I looked over my shoulder and could see Natalia heading towards us, waving her hands in the air with a huge grin on her face. Behind her followed Ramon and Charlotte.

"Hey!" I greeted her and Ramon with open arms. My smile faded as I pretended not to notice Charlotte. "When did you guys get here? You look super cute!" I ran my fingers through the purple tassels that hung from Natalia's two ponytails.

"About an hour ago. We were hoping we'd run into you guys early." Said Ramon.

Charlotte eased her way from behind Ramon. "Good to see you guys. It's been a while, Amari." Her eyes hung to the ground.

I remained tight-lipped. I still didn't have anything to say to Charlotte.

"How about we head out before it starts getting crowded." Gabriel suggested, breaking the awkward tension.

"Then let's get going!" Natalia exclaimed, latching her arm on to mine and leading the way out of the lot.

The parade was taking place only a few blocks away from where we had parked. The massive crowds gathering up and down the block covered the sidewalks waving pride flags and wearing colorful attire. I looked around, and for the first time in my entire life, I felt like I belonged. Like I could be my true self, with no barrier.

The parade began, cheers echoed all around as five handsome men led the first float carrying large letters made of balloons that spelled out pride. The float behind that one had a throne made of sequins, where a tall drag queen holding a microphone sat. They wore what I assumed was an altered wedding dress covered in pink, blue and purple tulle's, with white fishnet stockings and a bejeweled top hat veil. They peered out into the crowd as the parade came to a halt. They got up from the throne, grinning widely as they fluttered their abnormally long lashes.

"Olá a todos!" They screamed into the microphone, waving their left arm in the air. "Gual de vocês pessoas queridas quer vir comigo no trono hoje?"

The crowd erupted into cheer again.

"What are they saying?" I asked Gabriel.

"They're asking who wants to join them on the float."

"Does this usually happen?"

"I don't remember this happening last year, but it sounds like fun."

The drag queen stepped down from the float, with the microphone still in hand. Their eyes gazed over to where we were standing. Natalia and Ramon joined the others begging to be chosen. The queen approached us, still wearing that alluring grin across their face. They held out their arm and pointed directly at Charlotte.

"Vamos mami!" The queen called for Charlotte to follow them back to the float.

Charlotte beamed with wide eyes as if she had just been crowned Miss Universe.

My eyelids sagged as I watched Ramon and Natalia, rooting for her to join. Out of all people, it had to be Charlotte. As the woman reached out to her, Charlotte turned to me.

"You should go instead."

My right eyebrow shot up. "Me?"

"You heard me. Go, you deserve it." Charlotte insisted, pulling me towards the float.

"Yes! You should go!" Gabriel chimed in.

My eyes lit up as the drag queen took my hand and pulled me away before I could even say no. "Wait, I don't even know where I'm going! How will I find you?" I called out to Gabriel.

"Don't worry! We'll meet you at the end!"

Seeing that gratifying smile of his as he and my friends cheered me on overwhelmed me with joy as I took a step on to the float. The queen guided me to the sequin throne.

"What is your name sweetheart?" The queen asked in their extremely thick accent as they held the microphone up to my mouth.

My heart raced as I sat, looking out into the crowd as people shouted in encouragement from the sidelines. "My name is Amari." I uttered into the mic.

"Amari, welcome to São Paulo!" The queen shouted, removing her top hat veil and placing it on my head.

Music blasted from nearby speakers as the floats began to move again. I looked over my shoulder, Gabriel waved, blowing me a kiss as I was carried away. Excitement raced through me as we passed all these beautiful people, filled with joy and love. My eyes beamed as I grinned from ear to ear. My heart had never felt so full. Being at this celebration, and on this float I felt like the center of the universe. I had unearthed a greater joy than any I had ever known, and it was incredible.

***

We made our way back to Natal in the wee hours of the night, worn out from partying it up at Pride and spending nearly a day and a half on the road. I just wanted to curl up in my bed and spend my last two days in Brazil sleeping my exhaustion away. On the way to my house we came to the same intersection we were at the first night Gabriel and I went out together. The corners of my mouth turned up as I looked over at him.

"This is the spot we were in when you first asked me out." I said.

"He faced me, smiling. "Yeah, it was."

I sat there, vaguely reminiscing about every moment. From the time I first laid eyes on him at Coloma, to the moment we kissed on Fernando. My smile faded as the pain of reality gripped my chest.

"Gabriel, I'm not ready to go."

The light turned green, but we didn't move. Gabriel reached over to grab my hand. "Neither am I."

He turned the engine off, removing the keys from the ignition. I unstrapped my seatbelt, scooting closer to him. He wrapped his arm around me, as I rested my head under his arm. All I could do was savor the moment.

"You never told me what you wished for. When we watched the sun set that night, on Fernando." He said.

"I wished that one day I could live openly without worrying about how I'll be treated every day. Even if I never get the surgery, I just want to live the rest of my life as I am. Without the fear of what will happen next."

"You will, I promise."

"I don't think wishes work like that."

"Why not?"

"Because we can't change the world, or other people. Only ourselves."

"I'd change the world for you if I could."

"I know you would." I gazed up at him as he lowered his head, pulling me closer as we shared a soft, drawn out kiss. "Promise me you'll come to the states to visit. We can travel the country together just like we planned."

"I need you to promise me something first."

"What is it?"

"That no matter what happens to me, you'll live your life for you, and no one else."

"Don't talk like that. I don't like it when you get like this."

"Just promise me you will. Can you do that for me?"

I let out a slight gasp as I inhaled, trying not to cry. As I tried to hide that I was suffering too. "I promise."

He held my hand, holding me tighter. A car pulled up behind us, honking its horn.

"We should probably get going." He suggested, looking at the car in his rearview mirror.

"No. I wanna stay right here with you. Just for a little while longer."

He stroked my hair with his fingers. "Then we'll stay."

The car behind us pulled around, speeding past us while we just sat there. Listening to the katydids rattle from the trees under the midnight blue sky. I didn't care how long we stayed in the middle of the road. All that mattered to me was that I had him, for just a little while longer.

Chapter 23

I took one last walkthrough between my bedroom and bathroom to make sure I had everything packed before I left for the airport. I went over to my window to close the blinds. I pulled the string back and forth, thinking about the night I snuck Gabriel in. A small smile hung from my lips as I chuckled silently. I was going to miss this place, and all the memories I'd be leaving behind. My father appeared at the door, peeking his head in.

"Are you all good to go?" He asked, coming inside.

"Yeah, I'm just making sure I have everything." I walked over to my suitcases, checking all the zippers and stuffing the last of my make-up brushes in the front pocket.

"I can't believe the summer flew by so fast. Seems like it was only yesterday that I was getting the room ready for you before I picked you up at the airport." He traced the edge of the purple comforter, as he sat down on the bed.

"Yeah, time really flew. I'm gonna miss it here." I went over to take a seat next to him. "But I'm gonna miss you, most of all."

"I'm gonna miss you more, baby girl." He reached around to hug me, his embrace warm and tender. Just like when he would hug me when I was little. "I'm happy that I got to spend this time with you. I'm blessed to have you as a daughter."

"Daddy stop, you're gonna make me cry and I haven't even said goodbye to Gabriel yet." I joked, wiping the corners of my eyes.

"I'm sorry sweetie." We both laughed, he kissed my cheek.

"No, it's fine. I love you dad."

"I love you too."

He got up to grab my suitcases as we headed out to the car. We went outside, Gabriel, Miss Marcia and Charlotte had just arrived to see me before I left. Ramon and Natalia couldn't come, but we got to say our goodbyes the night before when we all went out for drinks. Charlotte approached me first, hugging me with a tight grip like I was leaving for war.

"I'm gonna miss you Amari! I leave the Corp next year, maybe we can connect again when I'm back in the states?" She suggested eagerly.

"Maybe." While my trust in our friendship hadn't been fully restored, I had no hate in my heart for her. Despite our issues, we had some good times together. I'd be lying if I said I wouldn't miss her, not even a little. "Goodbye Charlotte."

"Deus te abençoe! God Bless you Amari, have a safe trip back home!" Miss Marcia welcomed me with open arms. "I'll miss having you around in the garden. I hope to see you again soon!"

"I'll visit again! I promise!"

"I'm looking forward to it. You'll always have a home here. Take care darling and remember what I told you." She winked, placing gentle kisses on both sides of my face.

Gabriel inched closer towards me, carrying a small box in his hand. I could feel my heart breaking before we even said a word.

"I've got a gift for you." He handed to box to me. "But, don't open it until you leave."

"What is it?" I asked, observing it.

"You'll see." His hands held the sides of my arms, moving in to hug me tightly. I clutched the box under one arm so I could hold him with the other. His chin rested on top of my head. His arms clenched me tighter. I tried my hardest to hold it together, but I couldn't.

"I love you." I could feel the lump in my throat as my voice cracked. Sorrow shredding me on the inside.

"I love you too, Amari." We faced each other, he wiped my tears with his thumbs. "This isn't goodbye."

"I know." I sniffled. "See you next time."

"Yeah, next time." He said, smiling through the pain. I could see the heartache in his glossy eyes as we shared one last kiss.

My father started the car, Gabriel walked me over opening the door for me as I got inside. We held hands through the open window, taking in these last few moments together.

"Call me." He said.

"I will."

He kissed my hand, as we parted ways. I watched him and the others from the window, waving as we drove away. I inhaled and exhaled to collect myself, drying my eyes with the back of my hand. The box Gabriel gave me, sat on my lap.

"What's in it?" My father asked.

"I don't know." I removed the lid, and there was a white folded paper with two small papers on top of it. I unfolded the first one, it was a letter from Gabriel:

I told you I'd change the world for you if I could. Everything in this box is yours now.

Love, Gabriel

My brows drew together as I reached in to grab the other paper. I turned it over, and to my surprise, it was a money transfer receipt for six thousand U.S. dollars. The recipient was listed as my mother. The money had been wired to her bank account, for me. I covered my mouth as I stared at it, overwhelmed with joy and surprise at the same time. I pulled out the folded paper that sat at the bottom. It was thick, almost like a thin cloth. As I began to unfold it, I could see the print. It was his map. The one he had on the wall in this room. A weight settled on my heart as I folded it back, placing everything back inside the box as putting the lid back on.

"He must've given you a really nice gift." My father said.

I smiled. "He gave me everything."

Epilogue

In April of that following year, my life changed forever. After six months and working two jobs, I was able to save six grand, which including the money Gabriel had given me, was enough money to cover my surgery. My mother found an affordable surgeon in Canada that was recommended by one of the trans sex workers who was a regular at the clinic where she worked. I was finally able to get my vaginoplasty procedure. The grueling months that followed during my recovery were nothing like what I expected. But despite the constant dilating that consumed my days accompanied by unbearable soreness, I wouldn't have traded it for anything. I felt whole, like the part of me that was missing had finally been found. My father had taken time off from work to be there for me during my procedure and while I recovered. I wasn't prepared for the emotional toll my surgery would have on me.

There were days where I cried, battling slight dysmorphia and depression because I missed Gabriel so much. After the first month, the pain started going away and I didn't have to dilate as much, which was a relief. I could actually enjoy spending quality time with my parents. Having them both around made me feel like I was a kid again, and for the first time in a long time, my life felt complete.

Two months post-surgery, and I was feeling better just in time for my 20th birthday. I stood in my bedroom mirror, admiring my new high-rise Parasuco jeans that my mom bought me. Not having to tuck anymore, I had the confidence to wear anything I wanted now. I no longer had to worry about strangers seeing my bulge or having to wear shorts over my bathing suits. For most people, they were just a pair of jeans. But for me, they marked the beginning of a new life, My new life.

There was a knock on my door. "Hey honey, are you busy?" My father asked.

"No, come in." I walked over to sit at the end of my bed as he opened the door.

"Look at you! Love the outfit." He complimented, walking over to take a seat next to me. "Happy birthday baby girl." He planted a kiss on my forehead.

"Thanks dad." I leaned in to hug him.

"So, how are you feeling this morning?"

"Good." I sighed heavily, forcing a smile with pressed lips.

"It doesn't sound like it. What's wrong?"

"I miss Gabriel. I wish he was here."

My father held me closer, rubbing my shoulder. "You know he would've been here if he could've."

"I know. But it's still hard." I hung my head, suddenly in no mood to celebrate my birthday.

"Amari, you know I love you." My father lifted my chin, forcing my eyes back to his. "Your happiness matters to me more than anything else in this world. Don't ever forget it."

"I know daddy." I cracked a smile to lighten my mood.

"Now come downstairs, your mom and I still have gifts for you." he got up, heading out of my room as I followed behind.

I descended down the stairs, only getting halfway when I noticed my mother sitting on the sofa, grinning widely at me. Sitting next to her, was Gabriel. He looked up at me, and a wave of emotions hit me all at once as I stood there, unable to move.

"Gabriel…" My breath caught as my mind tried to process what my heart was feeling.

"Amari, it's so good to see you again." He stood up, that irresistible smile of his lit up the room, as he made his way over to me.

I ran the rest of the way down, casting my arms over his shoulders. My heart felt light as he pulled me close. Despite the heaviness in my stomach, it fluttered at the feeling of him pressed against me.

"I can't believe it's really you." I got choked up as my eyes filled with tears of joy. My hands brushed the sides of his face, touching him as if he weren't real. His hair was shorter now, which added a few years to his face. But he was still just as beautiful as he was the last time we saw each other.

"You have no idea how much I've missed you. I'm sorry I couldn't be here during your surgery, and for not telling you I was coming."

"I wanted it to be a surprise. Happy birthday baby." My father said.

"How about we give them some privacy." My mother suggested, as she and my father headed into the kitchen.

Gabriel and I had kept in touch over the phone, but nothing compared to having him here with me. I still couldn't believe it.

"How long are you here for?" I asked.

"A month. I cleared everything with my doctor to make sure it was safe for me to come, so I'll be okay." He assured me.

"I'm so glad you're here. There's so much to do, I don't even know where to start."

"You still have the map I gave you?"

"Of course, I do." I smiled, my heart fluttering as I kissed him. Slowly and softly, being reunited with his touch comforted me in ways that words never could.

I remembered what Miss Marcia told me. About how everything in life happens for a reason. I understood it now. It was the power of love that brought us here, in this moment. With our future together within its walls, now seeming a little less bleak.

Long ago I thought
i didn't know what love was
a passing thought, I was
now I can feel it's joy
love.

A poem from my poetry book "Sweet Oleander"

ABOUT THE AUTHOR

Born and raised in the Washington D.C. area, writing has been a passion of mine since I was young. I started writing my first book, 'My Colorblind Rainbow' in 2013. In 2017, I decided to continue writing, taking a leap of faith and following my dreams of publishing my first book which made the 'In the Margins Award Long List' for YA fiction 2018. I launched **Hardy Publications** in September of 2017, working as a freelance ghostwriter, author, and literary blogger. I also use my platform to raise awareness for different charities and non-profit organizations, donating a portion of my book royalties to help others in need.

Thanks for reading!

Check out my other books
My Colorblind Rainbow
River's Moonlight
The Coldest Moon
Mahogany Tales
Sweet Oleander
I Had a Dream About You

www.ingramcontent.com/pod-product-compliance
Lightning Source LLC
Chambersburg PA
CBHW051945170626
46808CB00007B/2493